CLAIMING HER INNOCENCE

A BILLIONAIRE FRIENDS TO LOVERS ROMANCE

HAPPILY EVER BILLIONAIRES
BOOK TWO

VIVIAN WOOD

AUTHOR'S COPYRIGHT

CLAIMING HER INNOCENCE

1

RYAN

NINETEEN YEARS AGO

*H*e still wasn't used to this. Last year it had been called recess, and it happened three times each day. But now? Now it was middle school, and they were all supposed to be more grown up, so it was "break" instead of recess and the lunch hour extended a full sixty minutes.

For the past six years, Ryan had navigated his ideal path to getting through each day. Honing how to spend the fifteen-minute recesses morning and afternoon had taken some time, and filling those thirty-minute lunches had also required some finesse. But still, he'd managed. And now this.

Someone had figured out that sixth graders still needed some semblance of play. There was a basketball court with weathered balls they could check out. An aging tetherball pole nobody played with any gusto. The track was open during lunch, too. But none of these interested him. It was enough getting through PE without everyone laughing at him.

Please, make the time move faster. When he checked the clock, the hands moved at an achingly slow speed.

Everything moved slow in middle school. The two friends he'd cultivated last year were gone—placed in different schools thanks to an arbitrary divide of the city. At least lunchtime no longer required assigned seating in the cafeteria, and that was some kind of freedom. He was hellbent on eating lunch outside away from the judgmental eyes of his peers, for as long as the autumn weather remained somewhat warm.

Who's that? A girl with pretty, cascading dark blonde hair and striking green eyes he could make out even from a distance walked through the double doors. She carried a bright orange tray from the cafeteria and glanced around the courtyard like a new and exotic animal dumped in the local city zoo. *Why's she wearing that?* With her white turtleneck and long wool pants, Ryan was hot just looking at her. His own thin T-shirt and mesh shorts still had him sweltering.

The sun demanded he squint. It was an Indian summer, and she was completely out of place. *Is she allergic to the sun?* She'd circled the courtyard once already, eyed peeled for a vacant seat. He'd already moved his stack of books to the floor. It was clear she could sit next to him, but she avoided his gaze and jumped on a picnic table that opened up when a group of popular girls left. She didn't seem to care that they'd left their mess behind.

He sighed and picked up his sad excuse for a slice of pizza. "What you got there?" Ryan stiffened even as the shadow engulfed his plate. School had only been going for two weeks, but the voice was already familiar.

"Pizza," Ryan said before he even looked up.

"Pizza, huh?" Dylan asked with a sneer as he leaned down and picked up the soggy triangle. "Looks more like your mom's panties, don't ya think?" Dylan hadn't been at Ryan's elementary school, and he was still trying to figure out how best to deflect the bully. Ryan had been used to watching all the other boys in his class shoot past him. He'd gone from average height and build in third grade to nearly the shortest by the time elementary school graduation had rolled around.

"I don't know," Ryan said quietly. The phrase was usually a safe bet.

"I don't know," Dylan mocked him. "I think you do. Shit, you look like the type that checks out his mom's nasties on the regular."

Ryan couldn't bring himself to look Dylan in the face. The spray of acne across Dylan's cheeks was a constant reminder of this terrifying new world. Some of the boys, Dylan included, already displayed hints of facial hair. They'd pull at the little tufts nonstop throughout every class. When Ryan ran a hand across his face, he felt nothing but soft, smooth skin.

"What, you don't talk?" Dylan asked. He tossed the pizza on the concrete. "You shy?" he asked with a laugh.

"Dyl, what's up, man?" Brian, one of Dylan's minions, suddenly appeared. He punched Dylan gently in the arm, a sign of brotherhood Ryan had never known.

"What's up? What's up is this little bitch thinks he's too good to talk," Dylan said. All around him, Ryan heard the early titters of laughter.

Enough. This is enough. Sure, it had only been two weeks, but the pattern was already established. It happened every single day. Usually Dylan started it, but sometimes it was another bully. It had felt like prison, these first few days, and it was clear he was earmarked to be the weakling. He couldn't help it—his fists bunched up tight like they were out of his control.

Ryan was already swinging toward Dylan as he stood up. He heard his tray hit the ground as his fist connected with nothing but air. Any momentum was already lost, and the missed target shot him off balance.

Dylan laughed as he rocked back on one foot. Ryan saw nothing but that balled up fist headed straight for his face. The shock of knuckle against nose was stronger than any kind of pain, but Ryan knew that wouldn't last long. He'd caught himself with nothing but a palm and elbow when he hit the concrete, and the pain pierced through his hand like a wasp sting. A warm, coppery stream started to pour out of his nose, and he saw Dylan start to set up for another punch.

"What the fuck?" Dylan said as the full soda can hit his temple. It connected with a dense thud, and bright red fruit juice sprayed across his face.

"You think you're so tough now?" The new girl was at Ryan's side, a second soda in her hand—this one in a glass bottle. "Come on, then. Show me. I dare you." Her voice wasn't what he expected. It was lilting and feminine, yet cool and steady. She sounded years older than she must have been.

"What wrong with you?" Dylan said. "You—"

"Try me, and I'll show you." She tossed the glass bottle between her hands. Dylan looked down, and his beady eyes widened.

"You're crazy," he whispered. He clutched his head as he turned and ran away. The crowd that had gathered, that had been egging Dylan on, dispersed as if nothing had happened. Ryan could hear some murmurings as small groups gossiped over what they'd just seen. It was like one of those prison movie scenes where everybody was trying to figure out the hierarchy.

"Hey," the blonde girl said to him. She offered her hand to help him up, and he took it with his good one. He didn't want her to see how badly he'd hurt his right palm.

"Hey, uh. Thanks," he said as he brushed off his shorts.

"That guy's a real jerk, huh?" When she spoke, her full lips parted to reveal incredibly white, straight teeth, save for the smallest of gaps between her front teeth. Like she'd had braces already, but the orthodontist couldn't bear to have her smile too perfect. It was in that so-called imperfection that Ryan got lost.

"Yeah, well," he said. "I'm used to it." *Shut up! Shut up!*

She cocked her head to the side, curious. "I'm Poppy, by the way," she said.

"Ryan," he said. He felt like he should shake her hand, but their hands were still clasped from her helping him up. He dropped her hand quickly, suddenly aware of the heat of her palm and the softness of her skin.

"Bullies can't usually take their own medicine. At least that's what I've discovered," she said. "Trust me, I've gone to a lot of schools."

"How come?" he asked. He wasn't sure if he'd even be able to follow her answer. All he knew is he didn't want her to go.

She just shrugged and smiled. "Long, boring story," she said.

"I could use a long, boring story," he said. "You wanna sit?"

She laughed and exposed that perfectly imperfect smile again. When she sat next to him, automatically offering up half her lunch, it didn't feel awkward or forced. He didn't feel like a charity case, like he usually did when one of the more empathetic kids took temporary mercy on him. It was just natural. Poppy straddled the bench and faced him directly. He searched her face for sweat or some kind of sign the weather got to her, but found nothing. It was like she existed on a totally different plane beyond them all.

"So you're new here?" he asked as she popped open the soda. *Stupid. We're all new here.*

But she just nodded. "Yeah, but *new* new," she said. "We moved here from the West Coast. At least this time I started a new school the same time as everyone else! Usually it's in the middle of the year after everyone's already made friends."

"Yeah," he said. As if he had any clue. He'd been in the same elementary school his entire life, had known the same group of kids since kindergarten.

There was some kind of security in elementary school, and even though the other kids might not have necessarily liked him, they tolerated him. There was a sense of camaraderie when you were in the same group for six years. This was all new, and not in a good way. Poppy was the first good thing he'd encountered.

"So, what's your story?" she asked as she tore into a peanut butter sandwich. She didn't eat like the other girls, all tiny careful bites and hyperawareness someone might be watching. Poppy ate like she enjoyed it.

"Not much of a story," he said as she handed him half her sandwich.

"I don't believe that," she said with a smile. A tiny spot of strawberry jam clung to the corner of her mouth.

Somehow, he just knew. They'd be friends for keeps.

2

___

RYAN

PRESENT DAY

*P*oppy's eyes commanded his as she pulled down her shorts in one fluid movement. Beneath that threadbare denim, just as he knew it would be, there was nothing—save for that strip of dark blonde hair. She reached behind her back and unhooked the white lace bra. As the strappy material fell away from her chest, she smiled.

"You like what you see?" It was Sarah, Poppy's friend with the long, layered dark brown shaggy hair. Sarah's olive skin complemented Poppy's creamy complexion perfectly. Ryan felt his hardness pressed against his jeans. But when he tried to stand up from the straight back chair, Poppy and Sarah both pushed him down. Sarah's touch was soft and gentle. Poppy's was a little more demanding.

"No, no, no," Poppy said with a laugh. "It's called a striptease. You're not allowed to take any of the tease out of it."

"At least not yet," Sarah said. "Help me?" she asked Poppy as she turned her back to Poppy and flipped her hair forward.

Poppy maintained eye contact with Ryan as she unzipped Sarah's floral dress that barely covered her ass.

Poppy slowly peeled Sarah's dress down her shoulders. Her fingers grazed across her friend's bare breasts and made the nipples harden instantly. The flimsy material fell to the floor, and Sarah stepped out of it. She left her black heels on. "Sarah!" Poppy said. "You could have left something more for me to take off."

Sarah shrugged, smiled at Ryan, and ran her fingers through her own triangle of dark hair. "I didn't want to frustrate the poor guy more than you've been managing for the past twenty years," she said.

He kept his eyes on Poppy even as Sarah moved onto his lap and faced him. His body responded naturally to having a pretty girl on his thighs, and her hair tickled his neck as she kissed his jaw. Poppy stood behind her friend. Her long golden hair covered her breasts. "Show me," he told Poppy, and it was as if she understood him completely. She grasped her hair in one hand and lifted it up, exposing her breasts for him with those perfect pink nipples.

"Switch," Poppy told Sarah as she placed a hand on her friend's shoulder. Sarah got up without a word, and Poppy took her place. She straddled Ryan, her breasts touching his chest. Without another word, her lips found his. They kissed deeply, and his eyes closed. It may as well just have been the two of them. He felt Poppy start to grind against the fly of his jeans.

"Sharing is caring." Sarah's voice broke the trance. When Ryan opened his eyes, Sarah was right there, cheek pressed against Poppy's. He was just inches away from them as their tongues intertwined. Still, even as Poppy got lost in her friend's mouth, her hands continue to roam across Ryan's chest. Her hard nipples were impossible to resist. He lowered his mouth to them.

Poppy responded instantly. "That feels good," she said. "Harder." He nibbled on her breasts and rolled her nipples between his lips. Poppy's eyes rolled back in her head and Sarah moved behind him. Right as he went to slide a finger through Poppy's wetness, Sarah grabbed his hands and held them behind his back.

"No touching," Sarah whispered. "Not unless we tell you to."

*R*yan awoke with a jolt, drenched in sweat. *What the fuck was that?*

He grabbed the towel off the chair next to the bed and started wiping himself down. The ache between his legs was almost unbearable. *Since when do I dream about Poppy like that? And her friends? Especially Sarah, Jesus.*

Ryan glanced around the room, disoriented. It took him a few seconds to figure out his location. *Stateside. You're stateside.* The obnoxiously loud clock clicked from 3:01 to 3:02. It felt like the middle of the night, but the glaring sun streaming through the windows meant it had to be afternoon.

He pushed himself up in bed even as the jet lag clung tight. It was his new apartment, that was all. He was still getting used to all the angles and shadows.

All around him, boxes reminded him of his new life. *Is this it? A handful of boxes and a mattress without a sheet?* He looked down at his new mattress and could make out sweat stains already. *Well, it was nice while it lasted.*

As he moved into the bathroom to brush his teeth, he shook his head at the dream. Poppy was his best friend, and had been for two decades. And as far as Sarah went? He'd only met her a few times. She was pretty enough, but annoying as hell. Either he was hot for her and didn't know it, or it had been a lot longer since he'd gotten any action than he realized.

When he'd met Sarah for the first time, he couldn't tell what Poppy saw in her. Then again, people probably said the same thing about Poppy and him. *I guess you never can gauge a friendship from the outside looking in.*

He could only imagine what Poppy would say if she knew about the dream. She'd probably laugh. *Yeah. Or shudder.*

It wasn't like he'd never thought about it before. *Hell, you always think "what if" with a female friend.* But they'd been friends for so long. It was the longest friendship he had. There was a part of him that thought it would be almost incestuous. Not that he thought of Poppy like a sister, but what if that was how she thought of him? Like a brother?

It wasn't worth risking their friendship anyway.

Ryan spat mint toothpaste into the sink. As he gazed into the mirror, he couldn't believe it. He'd only been discharged from the SEALs for three days, and he was still getting used to civilian life. The complete lack of a schedule was throwing him for a loop, that was all. No wonder he was having these crazy dreams.

He pulled on his jersey shorts, a well-worn Navy T-shirt and running shoes. In the condo gym, there was only one other person and the elderly woman in a pink tracksuit didn't even look at him.

Ryan had the free weights to himself. Years of perfecting a lifting regimen meant he didn't even have to think about reps or rest periods. Instead, he could lose himself in daydreams and plans while he took his arms and chest through their Tuesday workout.

Poppy didn't even know he was coming home, and he had the whole thing planned out. He'd low-key found out her rotation schedule at the hospital over the past few weeks, and Poppy had thought he was just interested in her daily life. Tomorrow, he'd pick up a bouquet of red poppies and surprise her at the end of her shift. It was cheesy, sure, but ever since he'd given her that poppy corsage in high school, it was their inside joke.

As he headed back upstairs, he ticked through the groceries he'd picked up yesterday. It was going to be cereal and milk for dinner unless he was up for another run to the corner market. He splashed water on his face, and dumped half a box of cornflakes into a salad bowl meant to serve an entire table. Ryan poured whole milk over the flakes as he called his brother Eli and put him on speakerphone.

"Hey, man! What's up? You back?" Eli's voice always brought him back to their basic training days.

"Yeah," Ryan said between chomps and slurps. "Just the other day. Jet lag is still kicking my ass though."

"What the hell are you doing? It sounds like you're feeding a starving Saint Bernard over there."

"Gotta feed the muscles," Ryan said between more spoonfuls.

"You still eat like you're twenty years old," Eli said. "That's going to catch up with you one day. Mark my words, you won't always have abs with a diet like that."

"It's cereal. That doesn't even count. Besides, I can't help how much I eat. I'm still a growing boy."

Eli laughed. "Yeah, a growing boy at thirty-something years old."

"Don't hate on the metabolism, asshole," Ryan said. It was good, this banter. He'd missed it since Eli had left the SEALs a few years ago.

"So. You seen Poppy yet?" Eli asked. He'd only met her a few times, but meeting Poppy once was all it took to see how special she was.

"Nah, not yet. I'm planning on surprising her tomorrow," Ryan said as he lifted the bowl to his mouth to drain the cereal-sweetened milk.

"You? Actually planning something without the MCPO making you?"

"Hey, I can plan," Ryan said. "I don't like to, but I can do it."

"Maybe getting out did you some good," Eli said.

"Maybe so."

"Sorry, I didn't mean to bring all that up," Eli said. "I mean, it's kind of bullshit they discharged you for that knee—"

"It's okay, man. Really," Ryan said. "Probably for the best. I mean, at least I finished that last tour with no serious injuries."

"Yeah. But, still." Ryan heard a rustling on Eli's end and a soft murmuring. "Hey, I gotta go," Eli said suddenly. "Duty calls."

"Okay, hit me up when you wanna meet up." It had been months since he'd seen Eli, and even though he missed his battle buddy, it was Poppy who he always thought of first.

Energized by the late lunch, he couldn't sit still. *Does it really matter if I see her today or tomorrow?* He knew Poppy was at the hospital until eight o'clock. What would an early surprise hurt?

Before he could talk himself out of it, he grabbed the motorcycle keys and loped downstairs. Poppy always chided him about his impulsiveness—said he'd surely get himself into trouble with it. But he couldn't help it. There was something electrifying in going with his gut. "You're an impulse marketer's dream!" Poppy always told him, and he took it as a compliment.

He just hoped the florist at the hospital had red poppies. Big, beautiful fresh ones that would make Poppy give him one of her world-stopping smiles.

3

POPPY

Nobody looked at her when she changed into a fresh pair of scrubs, that she was certain of. For Poppy, it didn't matter that she'd been changing with her fellow interns for the past year—she still got shy when it came down to slipping out of those blue baggy pants in public. The co-ed dressing room with its dark wooden cubbies, hard benches, and tough stained carpet that held who knows how many secrets was her dream come true.

She'd always wanted to be a physician, and now it was within reach. She readjusted her white lab coat and double-checked to make sure none of the vomit was on the lapels. It was her lucky day. The kid had only thrown up on her pants, leaving the white coat she'd worked years to earn crisp and clean for once.

Not that it was their fault, she reminded herself. She'd never had appendicitis herself, but had helped with numerous cases in the pediatrics wing. As an intern, she was still allowed to swing back and forth between pediatrics and endocrinology, at least when they overlapped. But not for long. "You're going to have to make up your mind," the lead physician always told her. The warnings had become more frequent in recent weeks.

She took one final look at her reflection in the locker. *I look forty years old,* she thought, and ran her fingers across her tired eyes. Greasy hair knotted up in a bun, no makeup and of course no jewelry. She'd never considered herself vain, but was still surprised what eight years of school and taking all those medical exams had done to her.

Still, she couldn't help but smile when her gaze wandered over to the photo of Ryan and her at a wedding last year. It was a miracle. One of the few times he'd been on leave and she'd actually had the evening off. In the photo, they clung to each other beneath a gazebo lit up like a fairy tale. She in her yellow, tea length dress like some kind of Grace Kelly incarnation, and Ryan looking ruggedly handsome in his tux. They were both laughing with squinted eyes and not a trace of holding back.

That night, they'd gone drink for drink at the open bar. Drunk on champagne, he'd asked her to slow dance, and it had felt like prom all over again. *This is it,* she'd remembered thinking. *This is how it should be.* Of course, it was the drinks talking.

"Isn't this romantic?" she'd asked him as she rested her head on his chest.

He'd laughed and said, "I guess so. If you're into this sort of thing. Rose-colored trellises, sunsets and all that." She'd punched him lightly in the chest, and in that moment she was reminded they'd always just be friends.

Sober Poppy was okay with that. It was their unspoken agreement, their pact. Friendship always came first. It was just when she had a drink or two in her that she started wondering, *What if?*

She was shaken out of her memory by the buzzing of her phone. Will. He always had a knack for texting her right when she was thinking about Ryan.

Dinner tonight? Something big I have to tell you.

Sure. Shouldn't she be more excited? After all, they'd been dating for three years. And he'd stuck with her through med school, when she was sure she must have been a raging pain.

Pick you up at 8. Wear something nice.

She shook her head and put the phone back in her pocket. Will was nice enough. Safe, her friends called him. And she didn't mind their life. He fulfilled the creative role as a screenwriter who was always working on something big. Not that he'd ever sold anything, but Will seemed satiated on those seemingly "close calls" he loved to talk about.

Plus, he'd never put pressure on her. "I think it's cool you're still a virgin," he had said when they first met. *Still.* She'd been twenty-eight at the time, and very aware she was past the cutesy stage of clinging to that V-card. By now, she was solidly in weird territory, and she knew it.

Will had accepted her situation because she'd dropped just enough hints about her past to tell him to back off. But nobody knew the whole truth—not even Ryan.

"You little whore." Her father had a way of hissing in a low snarl that froze her. He had a length of electric cord wrapped around his fist. "You think you're grown. Is that it?"

She was eleven years old and a lifetime of this had instilled part bravery and part stupidity into her. She was never sure which was which. "It's just lip gloss, Daddy," she whispered.

"What?" Her father smiled his wicked grin. The one she knew was a trap, but couldn't stop herself from inching toward.

"It's lip gloss. All the girls wear it."

The crack of the cord across her hip was electrifying. Instantly, a splitting blossom of pain exploded across her pelvic bone.

"Just lip gloss? What, you think you can just spread your legs for every boy that comes your way and ride off into the sunset like some kind of fairy tale?"

"No, I—"

"No is right," her dad said as he raised his hand to whip her again.

*P*oppy rubbed her hand along her hip where the scar had turned to keloid. All these years later, and she still needed routine steroid injections to keep the scar from rising. Every pair of pants irritated it, and ensured the scar was a constant reminder of her beginnings.

"Baker, let's go." One of the observing physicians popped his head into the locker room and barked at her. Like a dog. Sometimes that's what it felt like here. She loved it, loved the diagnostics and patients, but the politics and people drove her nuts.

She shook her head and slammed her locker door shut. As she started her rounds, her phone buzzed again. *Oh my God, Will, what is it?* She couldn't imagine what exciting news this must be. For Will to plan something that didn't involve beer tasting at a brewery with his boring friends meant it was serious.

Poppy was digging for her phone, head tucked down, and didn't even notice the big man in front of her. As she rammed into him, she felt nothing but solid muscle even as she fell to the ground.

"Women are always falling over themselves to get to me." Ryan smiled down at her and held out his hand. In his other hand was a spray of stunning poppies.

"Ryan! What are you—what are you doing here?" It was always a shock to see him since it happened so infrequently. Ever since he'd sprouted up in high school between sophomore and junior year, each time she saw him she'd think he'd eventually stop getting so handsome. But he bested himself year after year.

He pulled her up with ease, and she squealed as she wrapped her arms around him. He smelled incredible, a mix of cleanliness and masculinity. How could she ever forget that smell? It took her back to their high school days. "You smell like lemons and pine," she said, and blushed.

Ryan just laughed. "Thank you. I think? Though it kind of sounds like you're talking about floor cleaner."

"No, seriously," she said as she pushed on his chest. It was rock hard. "When did you get out?"

A nurse arrived right as she finished her question, eyebrow raised as she looked Ryan up and down. "The SEALSs," Ryan told the middle-aged nurse. "Not prison." Poppy covered her mouth in embarrassment. "Actually, just a few days ago. I was discharged—"

"Baker. I need you to confirm some data on the patient in 403," the nurse said, even as she kept an eye on Ryan's biceps that wouldn't be confined to his button-up.

"Oh, uh, sure! Yes, be right there. Ry, I have to get back to work, but—do you have plans for dinner?"

"Dinner? No, not yet…"

"Great! Do you want to go out with Will and me?" She bit her lip. "I mean, you can finally get to really know him, and—"

"Will? He's still around?" Ryan made a face. "I don't want to be a fifth wheel…"

The nurse rolled her eyes and walked away.

"Don't be silly! You won't be at all."

"Poppy, for real. That would be awkward."

She scoured the room and spotted Penny, a fellow intern, though Penny was a nurse and not a doctor. She was the closest thing to a friend Poppy had in this place, and they'd hung out a few times. Penny was likable, friendly, and most importantly single. "Penny! Come here a sec." Penny pranced over with her open smile and big, brown eyes. "This is Ryan, my best friend since forever."

"Hey," Ryan said.

Penny, usually open and outgoing, turned a deep red. "Hey. Hi," she said. *What the hell are you doing?* her eyes asked Poppy. But Poppy was used to this sort of reaction around Ryan.

"Do you have plans for dinner tonight?" she asked Penny.

"Me? Uh… some friends are hosting a LAN party, and I might—"

"Land party? Whatever, forget that. We're going to dinner tonight. Ryan just got into town. You should totally join us."

Penny's eyes grew even wider as they drank in every inch of Ryan. He smiled affably. "I hope you don't mind," he said to Penny. "I don't know anyone here besides Poppy. And Will. I'd sure appreciate the company."

"Oh!" Penny said. "Well—"

"Will's coming, too," Poppy said suddenly. "It'll be a foursome type of thing."

Poppy didn't think it was possible, but Penny grew an even deeper red. "Well. Um, I guess so?"

"Baker, I'm sorry to interrupt your social gathering." The nurse was back, and this time she managed to keep her eyes off Ryan. "But I really need—"

"Sorry, coming, coming," Poppy told her.

"It's okay, I'll show him out," Penny said as she smiled up shyly at Ryan.

"Thanks! I'll text you both the name of the restaurant in a few." She was grateful for Penny, but there was a gnawing doubt in the pit of her stomach. She watched the two of them head to the elevators together, and Ryan leaned down to say something to Penny that made her laugh.

What's wrong with you? Poppy forced the raw feeling out of herself as she opened the door to handle her patient.

4

RYAN

"Glad you could join us," Will said.

Jesus, I'm only a few minutes late, Ryan thought to himself. Actually, he hadn't been late. He'd just been sitting in the car for the past fifteen minutes trying to convince himself not just to go through with it, but to actually make an effort. It was what Poppy would want—all of them getting along. Plus, Penny didn't seem like such a bad girl. Quiet maybe, but that was alright.

"Sorry," Ryan said. "I got tied up."

"Yeah? How so?" Will asked.

"Will," Poppy hissed, and elbowed him in the ribs.

"What? I'm just curious what he's doing with himself, now that he's back and unemployed," Will said as he downed the last of a pint. "I mean, besides crashing other people's dinners, of course."

"Don't mind him," Poppy said as she smiled at Will. "I'm glad you could make it. We're all glad you could make it."

"Are we, Poppy?" Will asked. "I doubt Ryan has any interest in hearing about the big project I explicitly invited you out to share the news with."

"Nah, it's cool," Ryan said. "Tell me about it. That is, if you think I have the intellect to be able to understand all those big words you're going to throw at me."

"I'd rather not right now," Will said. "The mood's kind of ruined."

"Will, if you're going to be like that, maybe you should move onto something stronger," Poppy said. She tapped his beer glass. "You might be an annoying and obnoxious drunk on whiskey, but at least you're happy and tolerable." He faked a laugh, and she covertly rolled her eyes at Ryan.

She looked incredible. He'd thought she was beautiful earlier that day, with her hair swept up and without a whit of makeup. It was, well, it was how he imagined she'd look in the morning. Complete with loose pants like she couldn't find her own and had to borrow them.

But now? Poppy looked even more mesmerizing. Her hair was blown out and fell to the small of her back. She wore a fitted camisole and flowing skirt, but hadn't accounted for the chill of the restaurant. Through the thin material, he could make out every curve and line of her body.

"Hi, Ryan." Penny was to his right. Visibly nervous, she tucked the same strand of auburn hair behind her ear over and over again.

"Hey," he said. "You look good." Penny blushed.

"You, too," Penny said. Will just grunted and snapped his fingers at the server for another beer.

"Everyone ready to order?" the server asked. He was a wiry kid, likely a college student, with forearms covered in tattoos.

"Yes, now we're ready," Will said as he looked pointedly at Ryan. He ordered for himself and Poppy, who opened her mouth to clarify, protest, or something, but snapped it shut without a word. Ryan noticed and looked at her quizzically, but she just shook her head at him.

"And for you?" the server turned to Penny. She ordered a salad, as Ryan guessed she would. He'd never understood that. At the wedding he went to with Poppy last year, there was a sign at the open bar. *No great love story ever began with someone eating a salad.* He couldn't agree more, yet it was almost always the go-to order for women on a first date.

"I'll have the number nine," Ryan said.

"Sir, that serves three people."

"Okay," Ryan said.

"Oh! Are you all sharing?"

"Uh, I mean, I guess everyone can try some if they want," Ryan said. He smiled at Penny, "I have a feeling the Cajun tacos are going to be a little more filling than your rabbit food." Penny giggled, and he relaxed. It was the first real reaction he'd pulled out of her.

When the food came, the waiter pushed together a pair of the small, square two-seaters to make room for Ryan's spread. "Ryan!" Poppy exclaimed with a laugh.

"This is ridiculous," Will muttered under his breath.

"Sorry, Will, can you speak up? Can't hear you over here," Ryan said.

"Nothing," Will said. He pulled Poppy close to him and handfed her a small oyster from his plate.

"You know I don't like these much," she said, but she swallowed after two quick bites.

Will took her chin and kissed her while Penny furtively looked anywhere but at the couple across from her. "But I do," he said.

"Yeah, well, you eat them, then," Poppy said. She turned back to her own plate of gnocchi in wine sauce.

"I'd rather eat them off you," Will said. Ryan could see that his hand had slipped dangerously low under the table. He could only imagine where that hand was inching. Poppy slapped at her lap.

"Knock it off, I'm eating," she said.

Ryan worked through his first plate, then the next. At first, he offered each dish to Penny. After the first few times, she started nodding at him. He generally didn't like to share, but knew it was rude to let his date continue to munch on nothing but rainbow chard.

When Ryan offered Penny calamari from the third plate, she held up her hand. "I can't," she said. "I'm sure it's amazing, but I'm stuffed." Her eyes widened as she watched Ryan happily polish off the plate in a few big bites.

"I know," Poppy said to Penny, who didn't need to say a word. "It's amazing how much he eats. I always wonder where it all goes!"

"It goes to the eight miles I ran yesterday, and the eight miles I'll run before bed tonight," Ryan said as he wiped up the remainder of the rich sauce with the side of baguette he'd ordered. "And that's not counting the weights I'll lift."

"Don't be modest on our behalf or anything," Will said. "I mean, it's not like you interrupted a special dinner at a fancy restaurant or anything, so please. Do tell us more about your gym routine." Will had neatly patted his lips and pushed his half-eaten plate away.

"Nah, I'm good," Ryan said. "Why are you so interested in men's gym regimens, anyway? You know, I think there are websites for that—"

"Oh, hush, both of you," Poppy said. "Change of subject. Please. Hey, Ryan, I ran into Mr. Stott the other day."

"No shit, really? I haven't thought about him since senior year."

"Hey, language!" she said. She gave him a mock shake of the finger, but he knew her well enough to know there was some authenticity in it.

"Sorry, Miss Modesty," he said. "What's he up to?"

"I don't know," she said. "I pretended not to know who he was when he said hi to me in the store. It was too awkward. Plus I was covered in some kid's vomit."

Will groaned. "Lovely dinner conversation, Poppy."

Ryan laughed. "The last time I remember seeing him, it was actually pretty cool. He was in charge of 'babysitting' us before we headed out for Senior Send-Off, and let us watch *Star Wars* instead of working on essays like we were supposed to."

"Oh, wow. You know, I think I'd rather write an essay than watch that geek fodder." Poppy smiled as she picked up her glass of rosé.

"Geek fodder? I'm sorry we're not all as classy as you and don't watch *The Notebook* on repeat."

"Hey! *The Notebook* is good! Back me up, Penny," Poppy said.

"I don't know. I've never seen it," Penny said.

"I'm sorry, but as a screenwriter, I really can't put up with everyone talking about these crap 'films,' if you can call them that," Will interjected.

"Seriously, Will, lighten up," Poppy said. "We're just talking."

Will pushed his oversized, thick-framed glasses up his nose. The movement didn't shift how his eyes looked at all. *Are those even prescription?* Ryan wondered.

"I'm sorry," Will said, without an ounce of honesty. "But I did ask you to dinner to discuss my new project. And suddenly we're on some kind of mockery of a double date."

"Mockery?" Poppy said. "What do you mean by that?"

"Nothing," Will said with a sigh.

"You know, we'd be happy to hear about your project. But we're not going to beg you," she said.

"Hmm," Will said. "You know, I think someone needs to teach you some manners." His words were already slurred, but it took both Ryan and Penny by surprise when Will grabbed Poppy's head and plunged his tongue down her throat. Penny gasped beside Ryan.

"Will!" Poppy yelled. She shoved him off of her and the restaurant, loud as it was with people talking, quieted down.

All eyes were on their table. "I'm—I'm sorry about all this," she told them all as she gathered her belongings. "I'm sorry!" she called out to the restaurant. Table by table, everyone was slowly starting to get back to their own dinner.

"Poppy," Will started. "Don't make a sce—"

"A scene? You think I'm the one making a scene? I'm sorry, you guys," she said to Ryan and Penny. "I—I have an early day tomorrow. I think it's best if I head out now."

"How are you going to get home? I drove you—"

"You know, I think I can figure it out," she snapped at Will. "Goodnight, all."

"'Night," Ryan said quietly. Penny echoed her own goodbye after him.

Will stood up and slammed the chair against the table before leaving without another word.

"You know, it is getting late. I should probably be going, too…" Penny said hesitantly.

"Can I give you a ride home? I just have a motorcycle, but—" Ryan began to say.

"No, no! It's okay. I drove myself," Penny said.

"Oh. That's good. I mean, it's good you didn't ride with them…"

"Yeah," she said. "Well. Thanks. For meeting me." She hurriedly walked away.

"Yeah, sure," he said to her retreating back.

"Should I leave this with you?" The server appeared with a single bill in his hand.

"Sure. Why not?" Ryan said. He was still nursing his one and only beer of the night.

What in the hell did Poppy see in that asshole?

5

—

POPPY

"**W**ill! What was that tonight? I can't believe you—"

"Me? What's wrong with me? You're the one who ambushed me and invited all these people when I explicitly asked you out and said there was something important—"

"You know what? Just forget it." Poppy sat down on Will's tufted gray couch that perfectly matched the striped lounge chair while also complementing the brass-trimmed coffee table. It looked like it was out of a magazine on how to be an uptight jerk. Or from the guy's place in *Fight Club*.

Yeah. Probably more like that. She had a headache. She knew she should have stopped at her usual one glass of wine, but sometimes Will had a way of making her want a second just to numb his incessant nagging.

"I'm not going to forget it," Will said. *Of course you won't.* "And do you want to know why?" *No.* "Come on, ask me why, Poppy."

"Okay, why, Will?" Maybe if she appeased him he'd shut up.

"Because you're in love with that asshole, that's why." She stiffened at the word "asshole." She hated that word; it sounded like something her father would say.

"Who are you talking about?" she asked.

"My God, *Ryan,* Poppy, who else do you think I'm talking about? The waiter?"

She was dumbstruck. "Ryan? You're jealous of Ryan? You're being ridiculous."

"I'm not," he said. He shook his head and sat down in the chair, clutching a glass of scotch. "And honestly? I can't even be surprised. It's impossible to compete with that much history."

"We met when we were kids," she said. Why was she having to justify herself to him? Justify her friendship? "We've barely seen each other as adults. What with my being in med school and him in the SEALs—"

"Yeah, that's another thing," Will said as he took a swallow of the amber liquid. "The whole badass, 'I'm a Navy SEAL, don't fuck with me' thing he's got going on." Poppy cringed. Some words stung her like a wasp.

"It's not like that," she said. "He doesn't even talk about the war unless—"

"Oh my God, war," Will said. "His whole beatdown, underdog hero shtick is disgusting. Straight out of a crap screenplay if I ever saw it. And you," he said as he took another drink. "You just lap it all up."

"Me? What did I do?"

"Invited him to our dinner, for starters! You dragged along poor, plain Penny so it didn't look so obvious. That shy girl was in way over her head thanks to you."

Poppy hadn't even thought about that. She supposed maybe she had used Penny to try and soften the dinner a little bit. Make it not so awkward. But she'd thought Penny would be grateful! Everyone thought Ryan was hot. Penny didn't seem like the type to go on many dates, after all. "Maybe you're right," she said slowly.

"What was that?" Will leaned back in his chair. A smile played at his lips.

"I said maybe you're right. But I—I wasn't thinking of it like that. It's not like it was some mastermind plot or anything."

"I didn't think you had some major strategy to play with everyone's emotions," Will said. "But if you'd just stop and think for once, about anyone besides yourself… like me for example…"

"Will, I'm sorry," she said. "Truly. I didn't—I guess I've been kind of selfish lately."

"And it's not just about Ryan. It's work, too. You're always either at work, talking about work, or sleeping because you're too tired from work. Honestly Poppy, it's like you don't care about anyone but yourself."

"I'm sorry, Will. Seriously. It's just—I don't know. I'll try to do better." She caught herself before she could say it was work that was stressing her out. She didn't get it. All throughout med school, he'd acted like he was so proud of her. *When did he change? Or is it me?*

He sighed. "I'd like to believe you," he said. "I'll try, but it's hard when it's been like this for so long."

For so long? She hadn't even been an intern for six months yet. "I know," she said carefully. "I'm putting work before everything else."

He shrugged and looked out the window. *Childish. But at least he seems to have gotten off the Ryan kick.*

"So, tell me now," she said.

"Tell you what?"

She sighed. *I guess I'll have to drag it out of him.* "About your big news. I want to hear it."

"Oh, do you, now?"

"Will, please," she said.

"Alright, alright, if you insist. Remember that script I wrote two years ago? The one about the lesbian teens in Iran? It's been optioned by Netflix." He sank back into his chair like it was no big deal.

"Oh my gosh! Will, that's awesome! Amazing! I'm so proud of you." She jumped up from the couch and sat on the armchair beside him. His hands, the ones that had been all over her at dinner all night, didn't move from his glass.

"It's not that big a deal," he said. "It's just an option, not a guarantee or anything. Probably nothing will come of it."

If it's not that big a deal, and nothing will probably come of it, then why are you throwing such a hissy fit? "Oh, no," she said. "I'm sure it'll work out. Your work is incredible."

"Poppy," he said slowly. The ice cubes clinked in the crystal tumbler. "Do you even know what getting optioned means?"

She didn't, and she hated being tested. *Do you know what chronic atypical neutrophilic dermatosis with lipodystrophy and elevated temperature syndrome is?* she wanted to ask. He talked to her like she was an idiot. She was the doctor, not him. "Not exactly..."

"That's what I thought," he said. "Jesus, Poppy, you get all excitable over the stupidest things, and you don't even know what you're talking about."

"Will, I don't know what you want me to say. Do you want me to be happy about this, or..."

"What do I want you to say? To feel? I want you to take an interest in my work for once," he said. He set the sweaty glass down on the table without even using a coaster. "I don't want my girlfriend to feel like she needs directions on how to act when I tell her things about my work."

"Well I'm sorry! I'm sorry I don't know what an option is. You acted like it was this big deal, and then—"

"You certainly don't act sorry," he said as he cut her off. "I'm tired. I have to take an early flight to LA to meet about all of this."

"You're leaving? Oh, okay. Well, I guess..."

"Are you going to be here when I get back later this week? Or are you going to stay at your place?"

She had no desire to stay at his place with the idyllic, curated bookshelves and the dark wooden floors that magically never showed a speck of dust. Still, she was never certain what he wanted her to do. Sometimes it seemed like he wanted her to stay, and they'd doze off on the couch together. Other times, it was like he couldn't get rid of her fast enough. It was a guessing game, and she was too tired to try to win.

"I'm not sure…"

He rolled his eyes. "Look, if you stay, it's really important that you keep everything as it is. I know you like to sprawl out when you're back from a shift, but it's vital to my creative process that my space is—"

"I think I'll go home," she said.

"Are you sure?" It wasn't really a question.

"I'm sure," she said.

"Great, see you at the end of the week." He didn't lean up for a kiss, and she certainly wasn't going to offer.

"Okay. Sorry. Again. For everything," she said as she stood up and pulled on her jacket.

"Make sure you shut the door all the way."

As Poppy walked toward the elevator, her phone buzzed in her jacket pocket.

You okay? Put Mr. Cranky Pants to bed? Her face lit up immediately. Ryan had always had a knack for doing that. At least there was one man that wouldn't be mad at her, no matter what. She wished Will got her like that.

I'm okay. He's pouting and drinking. I'm heading home.

It's late. You okay driving? Want me to come get you?

She let out a laugh as the elevator brought her to the private garage. Only Ryan would think it was safer to take her home at midnight on a motorcycle rather than her driving her little sedan twenty minutes home.

I'm good, she replied. *Just wanna get home so I can wake up for 5:00 rounds.*

5??? You doctors are crazy. She liked how Ryan would regularly squeeze in the fact she was a doctor. She certainly didn't feel like it at the hospital. Interns were at the bottom of the totem pole. She got why, and there were doctors who had been at the hospital for decades. But nothing made her feel like all those years of schooling were pointless like standing around an annoyed patient and having a sixty-year-old doctor shoot questions at their cohort in an old school Socratic method.

Good thing we have mental therapists on call then, she texted to Ryan before she started home.

6

RYAN

He never got that runner's high everyone talked about, but there was certainly something therapeutic in long runs. He wasn't necessarily the fastest during his SEAL days, but instead squarely in the middle. However, he could pace like nobody's business. That meant he was always in the lead, and it drove the five-minute milers insane.

"Boy, you looking good!" He waved, a tad embarrassed, at the elderly woman who seemed to constantly be watering her flowers every time he raced by. He'd made the mistake once of stopping and talking to her. He was certain she would chat for hours if given the chance.

"Ryan, I got your mail again." His next door neighbor, a guy whose name he could never remember, called out to him.

"Slide it under my door?" he asked. "I gotta hit the weights before I lose my motivation."

"You? Lose motivation?" His neighbor chuckled and slapped his own mound of a belly. "I don't think missing a day of weights is going to hurt you."

He powered through leg day. *So fucking stupid going on a run before this.* He knew guys on his team who were hardcore into strength training. They lifted first thing in the morning, fasted, then pounded protein and waited thirty minutes before cardio. He admired their dedication—and research skills—but didn't see how they bulked up any different than the other guys. For Ryan, working out was always intuitive. He just did what felt good.

As he bounded upstairs, legs already strained from the grueling morning, he saw his neighbor had indeed stuck a hefty pile of mail under his door. Bills, junk, overdue notices. He shut them away in a kitchen drawer before he turned on the shower. *Out of sight, out of mind might not be the best approach, but right now it's the only option.*

Ryan stood under the pounding hot water and tried to guess what questions the US Marshals recruiter might ask. *What about my knee?* All the details were in his files, of course. *Would they really invite me for an interview if they were going to reject me because of that?*

It had been a long time since he was this nervous. Not since Basic Underwater Demolition/SEAL training, probably.

He rehearsed potential answers as he maneuvered the motorcycle to the recruiter's office. *No, I've never taken medication for depression, anxiety, or any other mental condition. My best training was the wet and sandy. No, I'm not married and I don't have a significant other.*

The building was unassuming—what more could he expect from the agency that was in charge of the Witness Protection

Program? He willed himself to stop shaking his leg nervously as he waited in the lobby in an uncomfortable plastic bucket seat.

"It'll be just another minute," the pretty receptionist told him for the third time. He tried to smile back, but it felt forced.

"Petty Officer Scott?" A gruff man appeared at the door beside the receptionist's desk. "Right this way."

As he followed the squat man through a narrow and dingy hallway, he couldn't help but feel like he was in trouble at school and this was the principal who was about to punish him with detention.

"Thank you for coming down," the man said. "I'm Lieutenant Stevens, and I'll be conducting this session." *Interview. Is it a good thing he didn't call it an interview? Or not?*

"Thank you for seeing me," Ryan said.

The man snorted. "I'll get right down to it. Your records are impressive. Silver Star Medal, impeccable recommendations, three platoons—you're certainly not lacking in your background and training."

"Thank you, sir," Ryan said. He sensed a "but" coming.

"Here's the thing. As you may or may not know, we're in need of solid vets for the US Marshals. The incidents in recent years? The suicides that were all over the news? That's done a number on our recruitment efforts."

Suicides? That hadn't come up in any of his research when he'd been trying to figure out his next move. "I can imagine. Sir."

"Because of that, we've been extremely vigilant about vetting candidates, particularly with regards to their mental health."

"Yes, sir."

"I see here that you had a patellar fracture. That what got you discharged?" The lieutenant's steely eyes sized him up and down. *Why is he asking me? Doesn't he already know?*

"Yes, sir."

"Huh," he said. "SEALs take every little thing serious, huh? Well, as long as you have the go-ahead from one of our doctors, that shouldn't be a problem. Nothing else, though? You know, up here?" The lieutenant tapped his own head with a pencil.

"Uh, no, sir. No." Shorter replies were always better.

"That's good. That's real good, son," he said. The lieutenant leaned back in his chair.

Am I supposed to do something now? He kept quiet. If this was some kind of game or test, he didn't know the rules.

"Nine months," the lieutenant said.

"Pardon, sir?"

"The hiring process takes about nine months right now. Used to be up to twelve, but like I said…"

"Excuse me, sir, but I'll be waiting nine months for a decision?

"Hell no, son. That's just how long the paperwork and all takes. And you applied through your local district. Smart, that'll speed it up. You'll have to go through the training academy within a hundred and sixty days of today, but that's nearby, too. And should be a breeze for a SEAL like you."

"I'd just like to clarify, sir. I'm in?"

"More or less," he said. "You'll enter at the GL-0082-07 level, just like all new recruits. After a year, you'll be eligible for a promotion. Sorry about that, it's the rules. Doesn't matter if you're a war hero or a nobody off the street. Well, I shouldn't say that. We don't really take nobodies."

The numbers swam in Ryan's head. He didn't know what they meant, but what did it mean that the lieutenant was apologizing? *That's gotta be a bad sign.*

"Thank you? Sir." It was the only thing that came to mind.

"Check with Pauline at reception. She'll have some paper-work for you, and can take it from there."

"Oh. Okay. Thank you, sir." Lieutenant Stevens rose and shook his hand, but had already sat back down by the time Ryan made it to the door.

"I see you applied to serve locally, too," Pauline said. "That's good! We could use some more like you around here." Her dark cocoa eyes looked hungry.

"Like me?"

"Like you." Her eyes never once broke his gaze.

He didn't want to go home yet—if you could call it that. It had been easy as a SEAL. Show up, and everything was already as it was required to be. It had been years since he'd actually had to put some effort into setting up an apartment. Instead, he swerved into a local smoothie shop where he knew they carried his favorite whey protein powder.

When he ordered, the skinny teenager who rang him up eyed Ryan's forearms. They were bronzed and taut, a surprise that jutted from the rolled-up sleeves of his formal dress shirt. "That protein powder really works then, huh?" the kid asked.

"It helps," Ryan said.

"Oh my God. Ryan? Ryan, is that you?" The voice behind him was oddly familiar. As he looked behind him, it took him a moment to place her.

"Sarah! Hey, how are you?" he asked as she went in for an awkward hug.

"I'm fine." He could feel her breasts pressing against his chest. "How are you? Poppy didn't tell me you were back. She's super busy, though."

"Good, good," he said. "It's been awhile. You look good."

"Thanks," she said, and glanced down at her tight skirt. "Work clothes, you know," she said with a laugh.

It was true, she did look good. In fact, that tight little black skirt looked even better than the floral dress she had been wearing in his dream. Now she was wearing a tailored little black jacket and some kind of pink silk camisole. *And what was she wearing underneath her clothes?*

"We should get together and catch up sometime," he said. He couldn't help the stirring in his trousers as he compared this Sarah to the one in his dream.

"Yes, for sure!" she said. "I have weird hours, but I'm free this Thursday night."

"Cool. How about dinner, then? Nine o'clock?"

"Sounds good," she said. "Do you have my number?"

"Yeah, from when I picked Poppy up at your place."

"That's right."

"I only have my bike, though. You okay with motorcycles, or should I get a cab for the night?"

"That's so sweet that you'd do that! But actually, yeah, I'm good with a bike. It sounds hot. What is it they say? Something about having so much power between your legs." She gave him a wink. "But I guess, like, this wouldn't be appropriate," she laughed and tugged at her skirt.

"Hey, whatever you're comfortable in," he said. "I wouldn't be one to complain."

"I bet not!" she said. "I'm sure I have some hot biker-friendly gear in my closet somewhere."

"Your protein shake's ready," the kid said in a small voice. Ryan turned to take it, and the cashier held onto the drink to force Ryan to lean in. "Dude," he said, and nodded slightly to Sarah.

Ryan just smiled and shrugged. "See you Thursday," he said to Sarah as he left.

"I'll text you my address in a minute," she said. He smiled and watched as the cashier ogled her openly. He couldn't blame him. Every inch of Sarah screamed of nothing but sex. Surely she'd be wild in bed.

Yeah, she was hot. Worth overlooking her annoying voice for awhile, at least. Still, he couldn't help but wonder if the whole thing would be as beguiling as his dream without Poppy there.

Why the hell are you thinking that? He could feel Sarah's eyes on him as he climbed on the bike. He didn't care what anyone said—there was something about a man on a motorcycle that women couldn't resist. It wasn't why he'd bought the hog of course, but it was a lesson he'd learned quickly. He felt like Marlon Brando in *The Wild Ones*. Even when he'd bought it, the sales clerk had told him, "Better be careful! They're gonna be all over you now."

At the time he'd just laughed, but he'd had his first taste of what the man had meant when he stopped for gas a few miles later. "Ain't nothing hotter than a man and his bike," the gas station attendant had said. It didn't matter that she was twice his age and covered in faded tattoos. He knew right then this bike was going to get him in trouble if he let it.

He tucked the drink into his satchel and revved up the engine. Ryan had planned to enjoy his drink there, but didn't want to stick around for awkward pre-date talk with Sarah.

He ran over the Sarah and Poppy fantasy in his head. The more he thought about it, the more he realized Sarah was just kind of there as a teaser. The trailer before the real deal. Maybe this whole thing was a mistake. He'd been known to be impulsive before, sometimes with devastating conse-quences—like the time he ended up dating a girl who full-on stalked him for a year afterward.

He frowned as he headed home and shook his head. Images of Poppy with her legs spread open on his lap refused to budge from his brain. Even in his dream, which he'd always heard meant you couldn't focus on details, every inch of her had been in high def. He could even see the damp spot on his jeans where her wetness had overflowed.

If asked, he could deliver a manifesto on the shape of her areolas and describe in perfect detail their exact shade of pink. If someone asked him right now if he could have anything in the world, without hesitation he'd say he'd want to have Poppy's nipples in his mouth. He wanted to make her squirm against him, beg him to be inside her.

Ryan pulled up to his apartment with his erection raging against his jeans. He raced up the stairs, forgot his drink on the bike, and leaned against the couch as he brought himself to orgasm. The only things he saw when he came were Poppy's nipples and wide open pinkness from his fantasy.

His phone chirped, and he pulled it from his jeans pocket. It was Sarah with a text of her address.

What are you thinking about Poppy for?

7

POPPY

Today was a freaking miracle. As Poppy pulled her blue scrub top over her head, she was amazed. For the first time in weeks, not a single kid had gotten sick on her. Her feet ached and her legs screamed, but all in all it was a good day for once.

"Oh my God, my arms are killing me," Penny said as she sidled up next to Poppy.

"Your arms? Why?"

"Because I had to carry around the Jackson baby all freaking afternoon."

"He's adorable," Poppy said as she slid her pants down. From the corner of her eye, she could see the youngest intern trying his best not to look their way. It was getting more natural, changing in front of everyone.

"He feels like he weighs a hundred pounds!"

"Penny, he's two years old."

"Biggest two-year-old ever," she grumbled. "You got plans tonight? First earlyish shift in a long time."

"Not really, probably stream something."

"No plans with Will?" Penny asked as she stepped out of her own scrubs.

"No, he's actually out of town for work."

"Cool! What's he doing?"

"Meeting some Netflix people. They're optioning one of his scripts."

"That's great! It's so amazing he's a creative who's actually driven and found a way to make money with his craft."

"Yeah. I guess it is pretty cool." *Sometimes I need to be reminded of that.*

"You know," Penny said as she pulled on jeans, "Ryan's okay, but Will is a lot better looking, in my opinion. Honestly P, I want someone like that. Someone with ambition who will really take care of me, you know? I hope you know how lucky you are."

Poppy smiled briefly just as her phone buzzed on the locker shelf.

Missing you HARD tonight. Will's text came through with a bathroom mirror shot of him, seemingly naked, though only the top of his pubic hair could be seen before everything else disappeared below the counter. Classy. She was a lucky girl indeed. For a second she thought about replying, but pursed her lips and clicked away.

She scrolled through the messages and emails she'd missed on her shift. *Hey, grab a drink with friends tonight? 9?* She couldn't help but smile at Ryan's text. *With friends, huh?*

"Is that Will?" Penny asked.

"Oh, um, yeah," she said.

"Told you. Lucky girl."

Poppy checked the time—it was already 9:30. Before she could talk herself out of it, she replied in a flurry. *Just off a long shift now, but see you soon! Text me place/address.*

In seconds, Ryan replied with a smiley face and the name of a nearby pub.

*A*s she walked through the heavy wooden double doors, she was relieved to find her jeans and T-shirt were perfectly suited for the little Irish bar. She scanned the crowd for Ryan, and spied him in the corner with… Sarah?

Sarah threw a dart wildly at the board. It stuck to the thick wooden paneling instead. Poppy walked toward them, and watched Sarah pretend to be embarrassed and hide her face in Ryan's chest. With a frown, Poppy walked faster.

"Hey! Poppy!" Ryan called, and engulfed her in a bear hug. "These are some of my buddies. Josh, Manny, Chris—this is Poppy. And, well, you know Sarah of course."

She smiled and gave Sarah a side squeeze. "You all ready for another round? Poppy? I'll get us a fresh pitcher." She nodded to Ryan as he headed for the bar.

"I didn't know you and Ryan were a thing," she whispered to Sarah.

Sarah's honey colored eyes were wide. "P, I—"

"Hey." Suddenly Ryan was back, his arm wrapped around Sarah's bare shoulders. "Actually, I'm going to order a pitcher for the guys. How about the three of us get a real drink?"

"Sure," Poppy said before Sarah could reply. "Jameson, rocks."

"Damn, girl, you go straight for the hard stuff."

"Ry, please—"

"I know, I know. Sorry. Darn, girl."

Sarah giggled and smacked Ryan's butt playfully. "Whiskey for all!" she called.

Seated at a high-top, just the three of them, the tension melted away with each sip. "I'm going to order some appetizers, you ladies want anything?"

"Bubble and squeak!" Sarah said.

"What the hell is that?"

"I don't know. I saw it on the menu and it sounds fun."

Ryan rolled his eyes, but ordered it when the server arrived —along with three other appetizers.

"Well, here's your 'leftover vegetables from a roast dinner,' Sarah," Ryan said when the dishes arrived. "At least that's what Google says it is. But if you're in the mood for some real food, we've got fish and chips, Shepherd's pie sliders, and some Guinness bread."

"How drunk are you?!" Sarah laughed. "Are you going to eat all of that?"

"Hey, these are just the appetizers," Ryan said as he dug in.

"I remember the first time we had fish and chips," Poppy said as she dipped the battered halibut in tartar sauce. "The lake we used to hang out at back in school. Lake of the Woods, I think it was called?"

"That's right!" Ryan said. "They had that random little food stall right at the park entrance. Run by that crazy old lady with the bad perm."

"Yeah," Poppy said, and started to laugh. "Then there was that one time the whole class went when we were, like, fifteen? That poor woman must have gone through her whole inventory for us!"

"I completely forgot about that!" Ryan said. "Talk about stupid, taking a bunch of teenagers to spend the night in a cabin."

"Oh my—Sarah. Sarah, that night, I caught Ryan red-handed with Jenny Thompkins! They were—I mean, you don't know who she was—but they were making out in the kitchen forever."

"It was all she would let me do!" he said.

Sarah laughed. "The kitchen, huh? Naughty, naughty." She shook her finger at Ryan and stuck out her lower lip.

Poppy downed the last of her now watered-down whiskey and reached for Ryan's—largely untouched since the food had arrived.

"But me?" Poppy said as she took a sip of the Jameson, "I didn't snitch! Nope. Not even though they were kind of loud in there."

"Don't exaggerate, we weren't that loud," he said as he moved to the sliders.

"You were totally loud! You woke up half the class trying to sneak back to your beds."

"Ooh!" Sarah said as her eyes lit up. "I like a man who's vocal."

"Don't get too excited," Poppy said. "It was mostly them banging around in the kitchen then trying to be all sleuth-like coming back."

"Banging—" Sarah started.

"The pans, Sarah, come on," Ryan said. "They were all over the counter."

"You know, I even pretended to throw up? To cover up for those two who clearly didn't know how to sneak around."

Ryan put down the slider. "Pretended? I though you really were sick!"

Poppy busted out laughing, and Sarah followed suit. "It wasn't that big a deal!" she said. "I mean, there was no way they were going to believe I, quiet and nerdy little Poppy, was going to be downing the Schnapps. I guess I had everybody fooled." Ryan shook his head.

"Aww," Sarah said. "You have such good friends, Ryan." She looped her arms through his, and he didn't seem to mind. Poppy watched him even give her waist a little squeeze, and she let out a yelp.

"There's the squeak," he teased her. "I already know where the bubbles are." Sarah laughed and slapped his arm.

As Poppy watched the flirtations unfold, she felt a lump grow in her throat and a sadness draw over her. *What's your problem? It's not like you're into Ryan or anything. You should be happy your two friends like each other.* She made a face at the thought.

"Poppy? Don't you think?" Ryan and Sarah looked at her inquisitively.

"Sorry. What?"

"Come on Poppy, keep up with the conversation!" Ryan said.

"Some of us are coming off of eighteen-hour shifts, okay?" she said with a smile.

"Oh, my bad, big busy doctor lady. Here, have some of this beer bread. It'll soak up some of that whiskey."

"You go ahead and finish it," she said. "I have to go to the restroom."

"I'll go with you," Sarah said as she stood up and adjusted her skintight jeans.

"More for me," Ryan said. He removed his arm from Sarah and used both hands to dig into the cheesy loaf.

"P?" Sarah asked as they stood before the mirrors. She swiped on lipstick while Poppy tightened her ponytail. "You're not upset. Right? About me and Ryan?"

"Of course not!" Poppy said. "Don't be silly. I'm happy if you are."

"It's just—there's nothing going on between you guys, is there?" Sarah caught Poppy's eyes in the mirror.

Poppy smiled. "No. No way. I'm just adjusting, that's all. To Ryan being back, and finding out you two—it's a lot. But I'm good. I'm happy for you both."

Sarah hugged her tight. "That's great," she said into Poppy's hair. "Because I'm super into him. Always have been."

"That's good!" Poppy said. "Seriously. Ryan's a good guy."

"Do you think he likes me?"

"I think we should get back to the party," Poppy said as she picked up her phone from the counter.

Sarah linked her arm through Poppy's as they walked back to the table, now surrounded by Ryan's friends.

Poppy hung in there the entire night, even stayed through last call for the first time in years. But she just couldn't help that feeling in her gut every time she looked at Ryan and Sarah.

8

RYAN

ey, my friend's having a pool party this afternoon! You and S should come. The text from Poppy woke Ryan up. He groaned at the bright morning light that streamed through his windows. *If ever there was a reason to buy curtains, this goddamned morning sun is it.*

When he saw the text was from Poppy, any last traces of sleepiness vanished. *I have nothing but free time,* he wrote back. *Will ask S.*

Ryan called Sarah, though he'd much prefer to text. However, he was in that strange millennial category where actual phone calls threw women for a loop. It was an easy way to make yourself stand out.

"Seriously, P's going to a party?" Sarah asked. "This sucks, I have to work today. But you should go. Send her my love." As he hung up with Sarah, relief washed over him. Why was he happy the girl he was seeing couldn't go?

Ryan thought he'd get there early at two o'clock when he drove up to the address Poppy had texted him, but there were already cars lined up the street. *Is this for real?* The music blasting from the backyard answered him when he was still three houses down. He couldn't even find a sliver of space to park his bike closer, since the street was so packed.

It took him awhile to push his way through the crowded foyer and through the throngs of people smashed into the living room. The kitchen, the obvious place for a makeshift bar, seemed to be professionally staffed with bartenders whipping up frozen margaritas and daiquiris.

"You seen Poppy?" he asked a random girl in cutoff shorts.

"Who?" she screamed at him.

"Never mind."

Finally, he spotted her poolside on a lounge chair. *Is that Poppy?* She was dressed, if it could be called that, in the tiniest white bikini he'd ever seen with just a few strings holding the fabric together. From the other side of the pool, he had to admit—she looked pretty damn hot.

Funny, I've never noticed her like that before. Poppy had always been just his best friend. Sure, he'd considered it before, just like he did with every girl he'd known. But in the past, the idea of Poppy, well, it just kind of grossed him out. But today was different.

He tried to shake it off as he made his way through the crowd toward her. "This party's poppin', Poppy," he said as he sat down by her legs.

She groaned. "That's terrible."

"That's my specialty."

She sat up with a smile, and when she did he couldn't tear his eyes away from her tits. The almost nonexistent bits of material covered her areolas, just barely, and not well. Even though the suit was dry, he could make out the shape of her nipples. *Thank God I'm sitting down. It would be really hard to hide this awkward erection.* "Where's Sarah?" she asked.

"Couldn't make it. Working," he said.

"That's too bad," she said, and made a face.

He shrugged. "We're taking things really slow, anyway. It's probably good to not see each other for a couple days. Besides, now you and I have time to catch up."

"Catch up?"

"Yeah. You know, on what I've missed since I was last here. How's school?" he asked. *Stop looking at her tits. Stop looking at her tits.* She shifted in her seat and leaned down to get a bottle of water. The weight of her breasts shifting mesmerized him.

"Not school anymore, really. I'm an intern now. I get to be on the floor with patients, getting my hands dirty."

"You still interested in pediatrics?"

"Totally. I'm actually interested in pediatric endocrinology, which is a fancy way of saying that I want to help kids who discover they have diabetes or problems with growth or puberty."

"Isn't that kind of depressing?"

"I don't think so. Kids are so resilient; even the sickest kids bounce back so fast, and they're so hopeful. It's kind of great. Maybe not the best party talk, though."

"Yeah," he said. "How are your parents, by the way? It's kind of a trip being here after all this time."

Poppy bit her lip and shook her head. "My dad is supposedly sober, but it's not the first time Mom's said that. Though she's ever hopeful! I don't know, I don't talk to them much. How's your family doing?"

"You probably know as well as I do! Ever since Eli became POTUS, well, most of them are busy being plastered all over the news."

"So crazy," Poppy said as she took a sip of water. "President at thirty-five freaking years old."

"But they're good," he said. "Him and Mer are good. And, actually I can't believe I haven't told you this, Ellie actually settled down."

"Yeah? Wait, with that jerk guy the media caught hooking up with some other girl in a bar bathroom or something?"

"No, no—one of Eli's friends. Henry. I don't know if you ever met him."

"Whoa, age gap," Poppy said.

"They seem to work," he said with a shrug. "He's even moving with her cross-country so she can go to vet school in California."

Poppy laughed. "I always knew Ellie was headed for big things."

Her grin was enough to make Ryan smile.

"Hey," she said, "how about we get a drink and get in the pool?"

In the kitchen, she asked the bartender for two piña coladas.

"What?" the bartender yelled over the music.

Poppy plugged the request into her phone and held it up. The bartender nodded, then a few minutes later handed them the colorful drinks. "Extra strong," Poppy said with a wink.

The water was warmer than he expected. "Why isn't anyone else in the water?" he asked.

She shrugged. "I'm not complaining."

He wasn't sure where the time went. Almost nobody else ventured into the pool—the women too afraid of messing up their hair, and the guys uninterested since it seemed there was just Ryan and Poppy, who swam in slow circles.

"Another round?" The bartender appeared poolside.

"Another?" Poppy asked Ryan with a raised brow.

"That'll be our third," he said.

"Fourth," the bartender said.

"Why not?" Poppy said. "It's a party."

"Speaking of," Ryan said, "how do you know all these people?"

"I don't!" she said with a laugh as the bartender handed them more cocktails. "I don't know, word of mouth happened, blah blah blah. You know how it goes. Plus, I like pools," she said. "If my parents had owned one, it probably would have helped boost me up the high school hierarchy."

"Poppy—"

"I'm serious! And I'm not upset. I mean, I know it's because you kind of pulled me along with you back then. I'm sorry if I held you back."

"Held me back?"

"You know… with girls and stuff. I wasn't exactly the life of the party."

"You were fine, Pops. You were perfect." *That had to be the drinks talking.* "Oh man, how far we've come," he said, eager to change the subject. "Can you believe Eli's president now?"

"That's so insane," she said with a laugh. "I always thought Eli was a geek until I saw him a few years ago."

"What do you mean?"

Poppy turned red. "I mean… Eli got attractive, you know? He's not my type, but—"

"There's just something about Scott men, huh?"

Poppy's blushing deepened to a near purple. Ryan couldn't help it. *She's fucking cute. Okay, maybe I'm buzzed. Drunk even. It's not a big deal.*

"Hey, help me with sunscreen?" she asked suddenly. "I have this patient with melanoma. Just fourteen years old. Now I'm terrified of skin cancer."

"Yeah, sure," he said.

As Poppy ascended the stairs, he couldn't move. Her bathing suit was almost transparent. He saw the line of her ass, and when she turned it was like she was wearing nothing. *Stay right where you are. This isn't a good idea.*

"Are you coming?" she asked.

"I don't know, it's really nice in here. Can't you—"

"Ryan, seriously. I can't do my back!"

"Okay, okay," he said. He sat beside her as she worked the lotion up her legs, her tight stomach, and across her chest.

"Do me now?" she asked. *Christ, don't you hear yourself?* Poppy turned onto her stomach on the lounge chair, and Ryan got to work brusquely.

"Ow, a little more gentle. Please?" she said.

He worked his way quickly from her neck and fumbled a bit with the string at her back—careful to avoid the sides of her breasts. As he moved down her back, he traced his fingers over those two dimples at the crest of her ass. He slid to the flanks of her hips. *Was that a shiver?*

Poppy sighed, and turned one cheek to the towel below her face. What would it be like? Just once—to kiss those lush lips?

Ryan stood up to move down to her calves, and Poppy looked up. Their eyes locked, and there was something in her emerald gaze. His eyes moved, seemingly of their own accord, to her lips and she licked them. Ryan sat back down and leaned toward her. As he closed his eyes, he saw her own flutter shut.

"I think I drank too much," she whispered and jolted up.

You are a fucking idiot. Obviously they were both drunk, and Poppy wasn't sending him any signals. "I, uh, I'm sorry?" he stammered at her.

"It's fine! Really. Just… silly," she said. He watched the fake, happy host façade take over and Poppy started chattering away with people nearby.

"You okay?" he asked her after half an hour. She was fully committed to ignoring him.

"Yeah! Actually, my Uber's here," she said as she packed up her things.

"Oh! I could have taken you—"

"I'm good," she said, and gave him a quick hug. "Thanks for coming."

You are a totally jackass, he thought as he watched her weave her way into the house.

9

POPPY

"I think I'm dying," Poppy told the empty room. Her hangover had claws dug deep into her head, the perfect complement to the ball of tension lodged in her chest. *What all happened yesterday?* She could recall glimpses—her and Ryan in the pool. How he rubbed her down with lotion. When he leaned into her—no, that couldn't be right.

She let the warm spray of the shower wash away parts of her hangover and the sticky sunscreen from the day before. When their eyes had locked, and his lips had been moving toward hers... they had, right? She couldn't have imagined that.

It had sparked a curiosity in her, a kind she'd never felt until now. *What would kissing Ryan be like?*

Looking back on it, it was strange they'd never kissed before. After all, they'd had the perfect teen romcom setup. Best friends in high school, the nerdy boy who got hot and popular, and the girl next door who he finally sees as more than a friend.

Maybe it was just too weird to even consider. She got dressed on autopilot, yanked up the faded scrubs and shuffled into her ugly orthopedic shoes. *Wait, it's Friday. Friday!* She was off rounds today for the first time since she'd scored this internship. Having Fridays off was reserved for the seasoned interns. Maybe that was her now.

I wonder what Ryan's doing right now.

Guilt started to creep over her. An incessant, nagging voice in her head reminded her of Will. *That's your boyfriend! He's the one you should be thinking about kissing.*

She punched Will's name into Facetime before she could talk herself out of it. "Hey!" she said when his face filled the screen. "How are you? I'm—"

"Can't talk much right now," he said. "I'm on my way to a coffee date with another writer. James? Remember I told you about him? He's a big deal here. And, well, everywhere."

"James, yeah, sure," she said. The name didn't sound familiar at all.

"It's been crazy here, but in a good way," he said. He talked to her in that formal voice he usually reserved for her friends he didn't like. Which was all of them.

"How so? Are you managing to do any sightseeing?"

"Sightseeing? Really, Poppy?" he asked with disgust.

"Sorry. It's just I've never been. I figured it would be cool to—"

"This is a work trip, not a vacation."

"I know that."

"But I've gotten some good feedback from people I've met with. Lots of feelers out there." *Feelers?*

"That's great! Yeah, I'm—"

"Oh, hey, I have to go now. I think I see him."

"Okay, call me—"

She stopped when she realized it was dead air. Poppy pursed her lips and tossed her phone on her bed. *He's so self-absorbed!* How had she never noticed before? He didn't even ask how she was.

Why did it even matter? *It's not like you're going to tell him about the almost kiss with Ryan, for crying out loud.* Will was already crazy jealous. But in his defense, it wasn't like he was the first. Most of her boyfriends had been jealous of Ryan. She hadn't dated a lot, but the few casual relationships she'd had always involved a jealous argument or two at some point.

Will was just the first one who wasn't totally wrong. She'd never thought about Ryan like that in the past, but now... now was different.

A tiny piece of her wanted to know what sleeping with Ryan would be like. Kissing him would be close, but not quite close enough. *What's wrong with you? You've never wanted to have sex with anyone before!*

To distract herself, she buried herself in chores. It had been weeks since she'd done any kind of cleaning, and maybe her mom was right after all—it did feel therapeutic. Cathartic, even.

When her phone started to chirp, she was annoyed at how easy it was to break that cleaning-induced meditative state.

It's probably Will, wanting to brag about his super successful coffee date.

"Shut up!" she yelled to her phone, but it persisted.

Finally, she grabbed the phone to see what the fuss was all about. *Poppy, why aren't you answering?* It was a text from Ryan. *I'm really sorry about yesterday.*

She sat down on her bed and composed reply after reply. Nothing sounded right.

Take you and Sarah to lunch to make up for it?

Poppy smiled and shot back a yes with a smiley face.

El Pajaro Azul in one hour, he replied.

She couldn't help but dress up for the occasion. It would be the first time… the first time for what? For Ryan to see her in something besides wrinkled jeans, T-shirts, and a borrowed bathing suit?

Why not? She deserved to pamper herself from time to time, too. Besides, it had been months since she'd worn anything besides medical scrubs and jeans. She pulled on a coral, strappy maxi dress and wiggled on her wedge heels. It was casual, but eye catching. And she'd surely blend right in.

As she strolled through the extravagant entryway of the restaurant, she realized the last time she'd been here it was different. The new owners had really pulled out all the stops. The grand foyer spilled over with exotic plants, and she spotted a small mariachi band serenading table after table. In the center, right behind the hostess stand, a massive cage of blue parrots fluttered and squawked.

"Reservations?" the hostess asked.

"Um," she began, but spotted Ryan and Sarah already seated in an intimate, half-circular booth, cuddled side by side. "Yeah, my friends are over there," she said.

As she approached, her stomach began flipping. *Stop it,* she commanded, and forced the feeling aside.

"P!" Sarah said, and jumped up to hug her. "I heard the party was banging. I'm sorry I missed it." She stuck her lower lip out in a pout.

"Oh, yeah, you actually didn't miss much," she said as she sat down and smoothed the dress beneath her. "The drinking and sugary mixers and the sun—I had a terrible headache this morning."

"You just need more practice," Sarah said with a wink and grabbed a tortilla strip.

"Everyone ready to order?" the waiter asked, pen poised above a pad.

"Poppy just got here," Sarah said.

"No, it's okay. I'm ready," she said. She always ordered the same thing at Mexican restaurants—one chile relleno and a cheese enchilada.

Sarah ordered the seafood combination, and Ryan was briefly torn between two different grande combination platters. "I'll just take them both," he told the waiter as he snapped the menu shut.

"Both, Señor? You sure? I can have the kitchen box one to go—"

"I'll take both," Ryan repeated.

When the entrees arrived, they all dug into their food, and Ryan took up half the table with his order as usual. "This boy can seriously eat," Sarah told Poppy. As if she had to. "I'm scared to ever cook for him; I don't know if I could afford all the ingredients!" Ryan just shrugged and scooped another helping of rice and beans onto a chip.

Sarah laughed and put her hand on his knee. Poppy saw his reaction—he sat bolt upright and stopped eating. "Excuse me, ladies," he said and made a beeline for the restrooms.

Sarah frowned at Poppy. "Do you think I'm coming on too strong? I mean, I know I can be assertive. Or aggressive, or whatever. I don't want to scare him off…"

"No, no," Poppy said to reassure her. "Actually… I don't know." She didn't want to be put in the middle, or suddenly be considered the go-between for them.

Sarah laughed. "You know him better than anyone! At least stateside. Come on, you're his bestie. His BFF."

"I'm sorry, but I really don't know," Poppy said as she set her fork down. "He's… I don't know. He's different now that he's come back." She didn't want to tell Sarah what kind of different, or that she'd started to notice how hot he was.

"Huh. Well, I guess I'll either figure it out… or I won't," Sarah said. She picked up her margarita and licked a touch of salt from the rim.

"So, tell me. What's up with work? I heard you have crazy hours." Poppy was desperate to change the subject.

"Oh my God, seriously. These clients are driving me insane. The whole digital era thing really just means you work around the clock."

"Yeah. I get that," Poppy said.

"Oh, sorry. I mean not like you, not like a doctor or anything." Sarah fumbled to fix her mistake.

"No, it's fine," Poppy said. She smiled and picked up her own margarita. "I didn't—sorry, I didn't mean to make it sound like your work is any less stressful than mine. Actually, honestly, I'm not even sure exactly what it is you do!"

"That makes two of us!" Sarah said. "It's boring to explain, but it's a whole lot of bullshitting with clients. And clients in the fashion industry are the biggest assholes. How's your drink?"

"Not bad, actually," Poppy said. She looked down, and it was half gone. At first when Sarah had pressured her to drink, she'd resisted, and just the thought of alcohol made her feel sick after yesterday. But apparently, it was true what they said. A little hair of the dog does work wonders. "I wasn't trying to act all holier than thou or anything with the job. I blame sleep deprivation."

"Or a hangover," Sarah said. "Hangovers can be a bitch."

"Yeah, or that! I haven't drank like that in years," Poppy said. "I don't know what got into me. Just—I guess I had a lot of partying to get out of my system."

"Girl, you deserve it. I mean, you've been either studying or working your entire life. You're young! You're hot! You deserve to let loose more often. Give that coochie of yours some action from time to time, you know?"

"Yeah, well, I'm lucky I'm not on rounds today. There's no way I could have gone in and been even partially conscious. My liver isn't what it used to be."

As the mariachi band approached, a tube of red roses attached to one of the guitars, Poppy just had one thought. She couldn't wait for this lunch to be over.

One of the guitarists handed each of them a rose, and they both shook their heads no violently. "Do they think we're on a date?" Sarah whispered to her.

"No rose?" the boy asked. He looked hurt.

"Yes, roses!" Ryan slid back into the booth. "One for each of my hot dates here."

Poppy blushed and Sarah laughed. The boy didn't say anything about money, but clearly made the "donation" bucket attached to his strap known.

Ryan glanced at what was already in there—only fives, tens and twenties. He plucked a twenty from his wallet and tucked it in.

"Ryan!" Poppy said.

"Yeah, they're the most expensive roses I've ever bought, but it's worth it," he said. "How many guys can say they're on a date with the two most beautiful girls in town, huh?"

Sarah giggled and rested her head on Ryan's shoulder. Poppy held the rose awkwardly as the band moved to another table. *What do I do with it now? Put it in my water cup?* The petals were already dying, and it smelled like nothing but Mexican food.

"You don't have to keep it," Ryan said. She was embarrassed. He'd caught her unawares.

"It's fine," she insisted. *I just don't know what to do with it.*

"Here," he said, and took it from her. With a snap, he removed the stem and all the thorns, leaving just a two-inch piece at the base of the flower. He tucked it behind her ear. "Que linda!" he said with a smile.

She reached up and touched the flower in her hair.

"Do me," Sarah said immediately, and handed her own rose to Ryan. He obliged, and trimmed off the excess stem with a snap.

"Do we look like Frida Kahlo?" she asked him.

"Uh, I personally don't think Frida Kahlo was very attractive, so…"

Sarah rolled her eyes. "I mean the Salma Hayek version of Frida Kahlo."

"In that case, yes. Hell yes," he said.

10

RYAN

"Hey man, what's up?" Mason still sounded half asleep, but it was nearly noon.

"Nothing much," Ryan said. "I'm back in town, wanted to see if you're up for grabbing a beer."

"No shit. Back for good, you mean? Discharged?"

"Yeah. Bum knee. Been around too much estrogen since I've been here."

Mason laughed. "I'm headed to a pickup game in a couple hours at Kalorama. You can join, it's just a few guys from work."

"Work, huh?" Ryan said. "Full-on civilian lifestyle now."

"Yeah," Mason said gruffly. "I went the private security route after my discharge. It's good, it's cool. See you at two?"

"See you, " Ryan said. Pickup games during their downtime at training was how he and Mason had first started hanging out. Ryan pulled on an old muscle tee and jersey shorts. He couldn't remember the last time he'd gotten a sweat on just for kicks.

"Ryan, this is Mike, Hakeem, Javi and Curtis," Mason said. Ryan nodded at them. Even now, at the modest neighborhood court, it was clear they were all ex-military. "Ryan and I were in the SEALs together."

"Cool, man," one of them said. Ryan had already forgotten who was who.

As Ryan ran up and down the court, the midday sun beat down on them. "Fucking foul," Mason said with a laugh when Ryan came at him hard.

"What, can't take it these days?" Ryan asked. It felt good, the adrenaline rush and roughhousing.

"I can take it fine. You're the one with the old man leg. What's it they say?" Mason asked as he dribbled the ball between his legs at the half court line. "I remember the days when my knees were right and left, not good and bad?"

Ryan shook his head and smiled. He missed this, when it was just the guys. But those days were mostly over. He'd noticed wedding rings on half the guys' hands.

"It's hot as balls out," one of them said after an hour. "This Indian summer is shit. Y'all want to head out?"

"Yeah," Mason said. "I'm still hungover from last night anyway. Antonio's?"

Ryan had never heard of it, and plugged the name into his GPS. So much had changed since he'd lived full-time in this town. He noticed it more and more. Everyone around him would talk about events, restaurants and names, and he always nodded along like it made perfect sense to him. *Since when does anyone go anywhere but Georgie's for a slice?*

They each ordered a pizza for themselves, and for once nobody gave him shit about his appetite. Families that lined the restaurant stared at the group of big men in their pickup gear, but nobody said anything—at least not until they ordered.

"Dad," a kid whispered. "Those men ordered five pizzas. For here!" The dad shushed his son and gave Ryan an embarrassed look. Ryan just grinned and winked at the kid.

As they each tucked into their pizzas, huddled around the tables with the staple red checkered cloths, Mason started to grill him.

"So, what's up?" Mason asked. "You normally don't just hit me up out of the blue like that. It's not like it's the first time you've been back in town."

"I always try to connect when I'm here," Ryan said. Even as the words spilled out, he knew it was a lie.

"Bullshit," Mason said. "I mean, I know we're all busy. But this was a first. Last time you were on leave for, what, a whole month and I didn't get so much as a booty call."

"Whatever, man," Ryan said with a laugh. "I'm sure you're not lacking any booty call action."

"You'd be surprised! You should know how it is, now that we're in our thirties. The good ones are taken and the hot ones are crazy. Just gotta wait it out now until the good hot ones get finished with their first marriages, then it's playtime all over again."

Ryan laughed. Mason always talked big, and Ryan knew he got his fair share of play, but he wasn't really like that. He knew Mason took his relationships seriously. "You got it all figured out," he said.

"I try. So, how is it? I mean, being out of the service and all."

"Weird. I mean, I was a SEAL for most of my adult life. I'm still getting used to the total lack of routine."

"Yeah, I remember that," Mason said. "Felt like I went straight from my mom's house with her yelling at me to get up at dawn to some sergeant doing the same thing."

"I don't know what it is. Human nature, maybe, to want that kind of discipline and someone managing you."

"That's strange though, isn't it?" Mason asked. "We spend our entire childhood and youth where we just can't wait to grow up. Then when we do, it's like we seek out parents all over again. I mean, a lot meaner, tougher ones, but still the same kind of thing. You adjusting, though?"

"Yeah. I think so," Ryan said. "I check in with the VA team pretty regularly. They seem to think I'm doing okay."

"And what about the royal family?" Mason asked with a wink.

"Shit, man, I don't know. Eli… it's fucking weird, right? For your brother to be POTUS?"

"I'd think so, but hell if I know!" Mason said. "My brother's an electrician."

"With the whole Ellie drama over and everything, it's mostly died down. Nobody really pays much attention to me."

"You sound jealous," Mason said. "Don't worry. I still see the paps getting your photo in the tabloids from time to time. You fulfill the role of the president's bad boy brother with your motorcycle and everything."

"Yeah, I think those are slow days," Ryan said. "Honestly, nobody ever bothers me or says much to me. All that hoopla from the campaign days has died down."

"Probably for the best. That was some crazy shit."

"I wouldn't really know. I was deployed for most of it. I feel kind of bad, because I got to duck out of the insanity of it, but the rest of the family had to deal with it all—"

"Don't be stupid. You were serving."

"I know, but when I heard all the stories, and when Ellie was getting death threats…"

Mason shook his head. "I know they had to take it seriously and everything because of Eli, but I really think it was just a bunch of online teenage drama bullshit. People think they can say anything online and it's not serious."

"Yeah, maybe."

"But what about you now? You seeing anyone? Or…"

Ryan looked down and pretended to be engrossed in his slice. "Nah, not really. It's complicated."

"Ain't that a Facebook status option?" Mason said as he drowned his own slice in parm and peppers. "But for real. I'm pretty smart, you know. With the ladies and everything. I'm up for listening if you want to bounce some stuff off me."

Ryan hesitated. Mason was right. He had always been good with not just women, but the real meaty part of relationships.

He acted like a badass, but when it came down to it there was a lot of sensitivity below the surface. He'd never tell him that, of course, but it was why he was so quick to befriend him. "I don't know, man."

Mason shrugged. "What could it hurt?"

Ryan looked at the other guys, who stuffed their faces with gusto and only popped their heads up occasionally to wash down bites of dough with beer. "I guess. Remember Poppy? My best friend since we were kids?"

"You talked about her, yeah."

"I never thought about her in any other way, ever. Until now, since I got back. I don't know, something's different. Maybe she's different, or me. I'm not sure."

"So, something going on then?"

"No. Not exactly. There was this time, this moment I guess you'd say, at a pool party just last week. We almost kissed, but she bailed at the last second. Acted like nothing happened ever since."

"Doesn't sound that complicated," Mason said. "It was a party. People are drunk. She might not even remember that."

"It's not just that. There's also… she has this friend, Sarah. I never thought much of her. She's kind of annoying, actually. But she's hot, and we've been hanging out."

"What's your definition of 'hanging out'?" Mason asked.

"Dating, I guess."

"You sleeping with her?"

"No. It hasn't got that far. But, you know, we're 'together.' Maybe, I don't even know if you'd say that."

"But while this is going on, you got feelings for your friend. Right?"

"I don't… yeah. I think so."

Mason finished a slice and grabbed a napkin. "All I know is, if you've got feelings for someone, it's not kind to lead another girl on."

"I don't even know if I have feelings for Poppy!" he said. The other guys glanced up, but went back to their pies. "I mean—"

"Look, all I know is you've told me you've been friends with this girl your whole life. If you don't see yourself ending that 'friendship' anytime soon, there's probably more going on than you realize. Than you even admit to yourself."

Ryan sighed, and Mason clapped him on the shoulder as he stood up. "Maybe you're right, man."

"See? I told you I was smart," Mason said as he tapped his temple. "There's another game starting soon, a group of guys from crossfit. You wanna join?"

"Yeah, sure," Ryan said. He looked down at the empty steel plates and the oil-covered napkins.

Do I have feelings for Poppy? Real ones? How did that ever happen?

11

POPPY

*P*oppy dropped the shopping bags on her bed and slouched into the desk chair. It was like this every year. She never knew what to get her mom for her birthday.

She'd walked around the mall for the past four hours. Nothing she saw seemed to scream at her, "Me! I'm what your mom wants." Instead, she'd dropped a fortune on chocolates at Godiva, not even sure if her mom liked high-end chocolates. At the overpriced lotion and perfume store, she'd splurged on a sampler kit. Finally, she'd tied it all together with a collection of decorative, organic soaps in the shapes of various animals.

Poppy tore the price tag off the woven basket she'd bought at the store where everything was imported from developing countries and each item was handmade. After lining the basket with tissue paper, complete with images of peonies so heavily in blossom they looked pregnant, she started arranging the gift basket. If nothing else, at least it would look pretty. Maybe her mom could even regift it.

This is ridiculous. It shouldn't be this hard, or this stressful to go see your mom for two hours for her birthday.

As she put the finishing touches on the basket, she glanced at the clock and realized she only had thirty minutes before she needed to leave. Her heart thundered. *It would be so much easier if I had a buffer. Some kind of safety net from Mom.*

Before she could talk herself out of it, she scrolled through her phone and texted Ryan. *Hey.*

Hey, Pops.

Do you want to go on an adventure? she asked and waited. The ellipses told her he was typing.

What kind of adventure?

Lunch, burgers, I'll buy.

I'm in.

I'll drive. Pick you up in 10.

When she pulled up to Ryan's condo, he was already waiting outside. She saw him from a block away, could recognize the slope of his shoulders from anywhere. *I've never before realized I know him so completely, and at the same time it's like I don't know him at all.*

"Thanks for the invite," he said as he climbed in. "You know I'd never turn down a burger. Or a chance to hang out with you," he added.

She bit her lip. "Do you mind actually getting a burger through a drive-through?"

"Oh, uh, no. Why? In a rush?"

"I have to go see my mom in Maryland. It's her birthday."

"Whoa! Wait, are you kidnapping me?"

"Ry, stop!" she said, and slapped his leg as she pulled away. "I could just use some backup, that's all. It's… awkward. Seeing my parents."

Ryan raised his brows. "And why isn't Will being the sacrificial buffer?"

She looked away and kept her eyes on the road. Still, she saw his eyes widen from her peripheral vision, and he twisted in the seat toward her.

"Wait a minute. They don't know about Will? How is that possible?"

She shrugged. "Never mind. Let's go get a burger, then I can drop you off back home. This was stupid, sorry."

"No! No, I'll go. I don't mind going. I'm just surprised is all. But on one condition."

"What's that?" she asked as she directed the car toward their favorite old-fashioned drive-in.

"You buy me a double," he said.

She laughed. "Yeah, you're going to need some fortitude to face my dad." She smiled at him weakly as she put the car in park. A young girl on roller skates drifted out of the small white shack.

"Hey, y'all. You need a menu, or you know what you'd like?" Poppy loved the nostalgia of the place, even though it looked more rundown and dreary every time she came here.

"We know. A double cheeseburger, a kids' hamburger, and waffle fries with both."

"And a large vanilla shake!" Ryan called from the passenger seat.

"Large? Our large is thirty-two ounces—"

"I know," Ryan said.

The waitress jotted down their order and skated back to the double doors.

"I can't believe this place is still here," Ryan said. "I remember coming here all the time when you were in med school."

"The cookies," Poppy said.

"Huh?"

"You used to bring me cookies from here in the middle of the night when I was studying."

"Oh, yeah," Ryan said. "It was the perfect arrangement. A cookie for you, a double with extra cheese for me."

"You know they sell antelope and bison meat here now," she said.

"No shit."

"Ryan!"

"My bad, sorry. Sorry."

The waitress arrived, expertly balancing a tray even as she stopped and balanced herself with a single toe stop. "Your large shake," she said as she handed the monstrous drink to Poppy, who had to hold it with both hands to pass it to Ryan. The lid came separate. On top of the thick shake, a mountain of chocolate-drenched berries threatened to avalanche over the side.

"That's what I'm talking about," Ryan said. He tried to fit it in the cup holder. "What the hell, Poppy? Are these holders miniature sized or something?"

"Uh, no, they're just not made for economy-size beverages." The waitress gave her a knowing smile and skated away.

"So," Ryan said as he somehow managed to take a bite out of the mile-high burger. "Is there anything I should know before we get there? Conversational dos, don'ts, whatever?"

"Oh, I wish I knew," she said as she picked the rings of raw red onion out of her burger.

"Why don't you ask for no onions?"

"I don't want to make a fuss," she said. "But really, I don't know. I'm guessing they'll be on their best behavior with you there."

Even though her burger was a quarter the size of his, they finished at the same time. "Ready?" he asked. He grabbed some wet wipes out of her glove box.

"As I'm ever going to be." She pulled the car out of the drive-through and headed toward the freeway.

"Bumfuck, Maryland, here we come," Ryan said as he began working on the shake.

"Ryan, seriously! Come on."

"Yeah, yeah," he said. "How come your parents never moved closer to you, anyway?"

"They never loved the city like I did," she said. "Too loud and fast paced for them."

"Makes sense, I guess," Ryan said. "At least they're still together though, right? Your parents? That's a rarity these days."

"I guess," Poppy said. She couldn't tell him her parents were likely still together because the idea of divorce was just wildly too foreign for their small-town, Southern minds.

"For real, you don't see it that often anymore," Ryan said. "I think that would be cool. To be together that long."

"I don't know," Poppy said. "I think it's hard to gauge a relationship from the outside. Being married forever doesn't necessarily equate to happiness. I don't think."

He gave her a sideways glance. "I'm sure you're right," he said. "All I know is my own mom. And, well, you've met her. Totally self-absorbed."

"I mean, I don't know her that well, of course," Poppy said. "But she never seemed self-absorbed to me. Kind of all over the place, sure. But maybe she's just finding herself is all."

"Isn't that what college is for? Or at least your twenties? Or even thirties?"

Poppy shrugged. "I guess it takes different people different amounts of time."

"Maybe so," Ryan said.

"I mean, my mom? I don't think she has a clue who she is. I'm not even sure she's interested in finding out."

"But that's not unusual for her generation. Everyone had assigned roles, and that's what you did. Who you were."

"Assigned roles? Like housewife? That doesn't make it right. Or mean that everyone, or even the majority, was happy with that arrangement."

"Do you think your mom's unhappy?" The question cut right to the chase and took her breath away.

"I don't know," she admitted. She had a hunch, for sure. How could her mom be happy married to a man like her father? She'd never had a career, never had any real hobbies. All she remembered of her mom was her cleaning, cooking, and otherwise fulfilling the wholly stereotypical housewife role.

*a*n hour later, they pulled up in front of a rundown white stucco house. She killed the engine and took a deep breath. *Is it too late to just turn around and go home?* Every time she came here, although it wasn't often, it was like the house was smaller. Dirtier. *Did I really come from this?*

She felt a hand on hers. Ryan's hand was huge, and easily consumed hers whole. His skin was warm and soft, even with the calluses from the years of lifting weights. How had she not noticed all of this before? Surely she'd touched his hand before. He felt electrifying.

"It's okay, Pops," he said. "I'm here. I'll be here every step of the way."

She let out a ragged breath and nodded, unable to trust herself to speak. It felt good, his hand. Too good.

"Hey, you okay?"

Finally, she looked at him and nodded. They got out in silence, and Ryan came over to her side. He helped her navigate the gravel driveway in her heels. As she opened the little metal gate, it let out a squeak and groan. *I know how you feel,* she thought to the rusted entry.

As they ascended the concrete steps, she tried not to look at the cobwebs flanking the doorframe. At the poorly stitched curtain in the awkward diamond window.

Why did I bring Ryan here?

1 2

RYAN

FIFTEEN YEARS AGO

Just six more goddamned months, Ryan thought to himself as he pedaled his hybrid bike through the streets to Poppy's house. He'd been working under the table gigs at Georgie's and saved up for the past two years to buy a car. His mom had promised she'd cosign for a "reasonable sedan," but that wasn't what he wanted—neither her help, nor a lame four-door car. He had his eyes on a Trans Am, and the day he turned sixteen he was going to buy one for himself. And someday, a motorcycle.

As he pulled up outside Poppy's house, he jumped off the bike and let it fall into the small patch of grass out front. He started to shrug off his backpack and get ready to knock when he heard it. The bloodcurdling scream from inside shot chills through him.

The knob turned with ease. *Thank you, God.* Even as he rushed inside, he was aware it was adrenaline and fear that drove him forward. He raced through the little hallway, and glanced at the formal living room Poppy's family used for storage and a makeshift office. It was empty.

He ran into the kitchen and froze. Poppy's father was standing menacingly over her as she was huddled in a corner. *What is she doing?* It looked like Poppy was covering someone, like she was a heroine in an action movie.

Suddenly, he understood what was happening. Poppy was crouched over her mother. Her father's back was to Ryan, and her mom seemed to be unconscious, sprawled across the linoleum.

Poppy was sobbing, and a few words blubbered out of her. "Why? How could you?" She repeated the phrase over and over again. Poppy grabbed a tea towel from the stove's handle and tried to tuck it under her mom's head. When she wiped at her own nose, it brought on a fresh new flow of bright red blood. Poppy's light blue shirt was drenched in what looked like red rust, and her face was smeared in it.

Ryan couldn't move.

"You're both whores!" her father growled. He'd never heard Mr. Baker sound like that before.

"You didn't have to hit her!" Poppy cried through tears and blood.

"You're both—both you crazy bitches bring it on yourselves," Mr. Baker said. He staggered slightly and clutched a kitchen chair for support. Was he drunk?

"Stop it!" Poppy said, and held up a forearm. It was a warning. He'd only seen Poppy act like that on the day they first met, but he knew it instinctively.

"And you! You're worse than her," Mr. Baker said. "Fucking piece of shit whore, I see the way you look at men." He started toward Poppy, and lifted up a hand that Ryan didn't realize until then was holding a belt with a giant metal buckle at the end.

"Stop." *Fuck, was that me?* The voice that poured out of his throat was deep, calm and commanding.

Mr. Baker and Poppy both looked at him for the first time. "You mind your own business," Mr. Baker said. "And get the fuck out of my house."

"Ryan," Poppy said, her eyes big.

He didn't realize he'd closed the gap between him and Mr. Baker. All he knew was that he was suddenly on top of him. Straddled over the middle-aged man's paunch, Ryan landed punches wherever he could.

"Motherfucker," Mr. Baker grunted, and shoved Ryan off of him with a strength that shouldn't have been possible.

Ryan's head hit the floor, and Mr. Baker's fist landed squarely on Ryan's jaw. The shock stung more than the actual punch. Her dad must have had forty pounds on him, and Ryan had never been in a fight before. Still, his youth and sheer anger were on his side. After he took two more punches to the face, he kicked his way backward and out of Mr. Baker's reach.

Ryan stood up and caught him by surprise. Right as Mr. Baker looked up, Ryan landed a hit squarely on his nose. As Mr. Baker reached up to protect his face, Ryan sent an uppercut into his throat and followed with a hit to the temple. With his breath knocked out and windpipe temporarily closed, Mr. Baker hit the floor with a solid thud. He was out.

He heard Mrs. Baker sobbing softly on the floor. *When did she wake up? Did she see everything?* He didn't know if he should be worried or proud. Poppy seemed to be in shock. Ryan grabbed Poppy's hand and helped her up. Easily, he lifted her mother over his shoulder. She couldn't have weighed more than ninety pounds—a tiny little thing.

After he sat Mrs. Baker on the sofa, she was still moaning gently, not quite fully alert. Poppy looked through the doorway to her father's unmoving body, unconscious on the kitchen floor. The floodgates opened, and she started crying nonstop.

"Hey, it's okay. It's okay," he told her. *How the fuck do you know it's okay?* "Should I—do you want me to call my mom? I can—"

Suddenly, Mrs. Baker reached over and patted Ryan gently on the arm. She was still groggy, and her voice was slurred. "Nobody's going anywhere," she told him with a sad smile.

"Mrs. Baker, I'm sorry, but I think you need—I mean, some medical attention might—"

"Sweetie, you couldn't understand," she said.

Poppy grabbed his hand and shook her head vigorously. He knew better than to argue.

Mr. Baker began to groan in the next room. Ryan couldn't see him on the floor anymore, but he rumbled about in the kitchen and sounded like a wild animal. "Poppy, let's go," he said. Mrs. Baker leaned back on the couch and closed her eyes.

Without a word, Poppy let him lead her out the back door. They didn't exchange a word until they reached their special Mitchell Park bench. It was their unspoken secret place, even though it was out in the open. Somehow, even with the rolling lawn and joggers passing by, it always seemed like they were alone here.

He didn't know what to do, but when he wrapped an arm around her she fell into his chest naturally. Ryan pulled a bandanna out of his pocket and started wiping at the blood on her face. It was everywhere. It caked her neck and drenched her shirt. "Poppy," he started, "is this…"

She nodded. "It's—it's usually not this bad," she said. "Really."

"But, how long…"

"Um, I don't know. As long as I can remember? I guess?" She was halting in her words, and he could tell she was holding back. But he didn't want to push her.

"Why didn't you ever—I mean, how could I not notice?"

Quietly, she pulled her shirt out of her skirt and stood before him. Poppy looked around to see if anyone was coming. When she was sure it was clear, she lifted up her shirt and exposed her stomach. It was covered in bruises all shades of purple and blue. Some bruises were recent, and others were nearly faded away. She turned like a ballerina in a music box, and he saw rows of welts on her back. Before he could stop himself, he traced one of the healed scars with his fingertip.

"This is serious," he said, but Poppy just pulled her shirt back down and shook her head.

"It looks worse than it is," she said. "Seriously. I mean… he drinks. You know? And sometimes it gets out of control. He can't—he can't help when he gets mad at us. I mean, my mom and I, we have a lot of flaws, you know? It makes him mad—"

Ryan's fists automatically balled up, but he hugged Poppy tight. As he held her close, her hair flew across his face. "Your dad's a monster, and it not your fault. Or your mom's," he said.

"Ryan," she said. "It's okay, really—"

He held her tighter, afraid that if he looked at her face right then, he'd start crying, too. "No. There's no level of badness that could come close to excusing what your dad's done."

Poppy sighed into his arms. "I shouldn't have said anything," she said. "I think… I feel like I made it sound worse than it is."

"Stop it," he said. "I can't—I can't undo what your father's done. But I can promise that I'll never let anything bad happen to you. Not ever again."

He didn't know how long they stayed like that, intertwined on the park bench where they'd spend the past four years talking, laughing, and he'd thought sharing secrets. *How could she have kept something like this secret? How could I have been so blind?*

Ryan clutched her tighter, and started to rewind their years together. Little pieces of an otherwise enigma of a puzzle began to come together. The turtleneck and long sleeves on a sweltering day. The long skirts. The pained looks on her face so often when they were in PE and a dodgeball hit her just right.

He couldn't believe how blind he'd been, how stupid. His best friend was hurting, and he hadn't even noticed.

She felt both incredibly alive and powerful, yet so fragile in his arms. He'd hugged Poppy hundreds of times over the years, but it was always quick and in fun. Not like this. He felt like he was cradling the whole world in his arms, an enormous responsibility. He thought it would be over-whelming and terrifying to be in that kind of position, but it wasn't.

It felt wholly natural, like this was right where he belonged.

94

13

POPPY

*P*oppy knocked on the peeling wooden door. The doorbell had never worked. As she looked around the small patio, peppered with bags of newspapers and a ratty old welcome mat, a wave of embarrassment washed over her. She didn't want Ryan to remember where she'd come from.

Her mother answered, and Poppy's throat was instantly thick with emotion. Her mom looked much, much older. Poppy could still see the pretty young woman her mom had once been, the woman she remembered from her youngest days, but now the hair was solid gray at the roots and deep rivulets of wrinkles covered her face.

"Poppy," her mom said. Her face lit up—until she noticed Ryan. "And Ryan. I—I'm sorry. We weren't expecting anyone else for dinner—"

"Mom!" Poppy snapped at her. It happened every time. She was instantly turned back into a teenager whenever she came "home." She took a deep breath and tried to steady her voice.

"You begged me to come out here," she said coolly. "If you want to see me, you'll make room for Ryan."

Her mom's milky blue eyes shifted back and forth between Poppy and Ryan. With a swallow, she whispered, "Wait one second." She disappeared into the dark house, leaving the door cracked just a sliver.

Poppy looked up at Ryan, and apologized with her eyes. He smiled slightly. She couldn't get a read on him.

When her mom returned, she was wearing a strained smile, but opened the door to usher them in. "Let me have your coats," she said. Poppy slipped out of hers awkwardly. Her mom was acting like a butler, a maid. "Come, we'll be eating in the kitchen."

The same round, wooden dining room table from her youth was squeezed into a corner of the 1970s-orange kitchen. Her dad was already hunched over the table, halfway through his plate.

"Hi, Dad." He barely looked up at them, but nodded his acknowledgment to her and ignored Ryan. He seemed smaller, yet fatter, than she remembered. The monster of her youth lurked below the surface. Poppy could still sense that. But it was almost sad how much he'd shrunk. Almost.

"How was the drive?" her mom asked as she scrambled to set another place for Ryan. He had to shove himself into the farthest corner. A hook of old grocery bags hung over his head, but he didn't move to brush them away.

"Okay," Poppy said. Her mom placed three plates of piping hot food on the table.

"That's good," her mom said. She picked up a battered fork, from the same set Poppy recalled as a child.

From the corner of her eye, Poppy saw that Ryan barely touched his food. She took a few bites, but tasted nothing. The red potatoes were flavorless. The catfish didn't seem to have any seasoning. She pushed the food around her plate and made intricate designs.

"The neighbors," her mom said as she lifted a forkful of cornbread to her mouth, "they're at it again. It's the fourth weekend in a row they've had a 'yard sale.' I don't know what they're doing, probably buying junk from other sales and trying to make a profit."

"Hmm," Poppy said, eyes glued to her plate.

"And the Hubbards? Three doors down? They got some kind of beast dog that sounds like it's absolutely dying all hours of the—"

"You come to tell us you're getting married?" It was the first thing her father had said to her, and his voice shot her back to being five years old. He might have looked different, but that voice was the same. Deep, dark and always dangerous.

"What?" She was mortified. "I'm not… I'm not…"

The words wouldn't come out. "Dad, he's—Ryan and I aren't even dating…"

"Well, thank God for that," her dad said. He stood up and slapped his napkin down on the table. He loomed over her, and he was ten feet tall all over again.

As her dad turned and left the room, she looked at Ryan. She could feel the blood boiling below the surface, and knew her face was bright red. However, Ryan just smiled at her in a funny way she'd never seen before and looked down.

"Your father…" Her mother just shook her head. "You know how he can be. So tell me how work's going."

"I, uh." Poppy struggled to find words, and some sense of normalcy. "It's okay, I guess."

"Working a lot of hours? Like on TV?" her mom asked. The closest thing her mom knew about what Poppy did was *Grey's Anatomy,* and she was convinced Poppy's life was just as dramatic and sex-filled as the characters.

"Yeah, something like that," Poppy said. "It's not too bad, though."

"Well, that's good," her mom said. "I never understood that. Why the people who need the most rest, doctors and pilots, they're the ones with the crazy work schedule. Sleep-deprived, drinking caffeine nonstop. It's not good. You'd think doctors and pilots would be the people we'd all want to be well-rested!"

"Yeah," Poppy said.

"Well. As long as you're taking care of yourself," her mom said.

That's a funny thought. Take care of myself? Like you were supposed to take care of me for all those years?

She watched her mom finish the plate. She was frailer than the last time, though it wasn't noticeable at first. Dressed in a button-up shirt and jeans, Poppy focused on her mother's hands. They looked like how she remembered her grandmother's hands, with blue veins visible and small knots at the knuckles. They were old woman hands.

Poppy looked down at her own hands and tried to see what they'd turn into, but there was nothing of her mom in her.

Her own hands showcased a sloppy at-home manicure. At least she'd tried. One of the attending physicians had told her, told all the women, that manicures made the patients trust you more.

Nobody wanted a doctor who looked like they worked at a mechanic shop on the side.

"And that fluorescent light you must deal with all day—"

Her mom started to pick up all their plates. She didn't say a word about Ryan and Poppy not eating. "I'll get that," Poppy said, and grabbed the plates.

"Oh! Well, thank you dear," her mom said and sat back down.

Poppy scraped the two full plates into the bin and rinsed the chipped plates in the sink. Her back was to her mom and Ryan at the table, and the room was silent save for the spray of water. "We should probably get going," she said to the wall. She couldn't bear to look her mom in the face.

"So soon." It wasn't a question. *Was that defeat she heard in her mom's voice?*

"I have an early shift tomorrow," she said. "And a bunch of stuff to do at home first."

"I just hope you're not so busy that you don't have time for yourself," her mom said.

Poppy didn't reply. *Time for myself? To do what? Get married?*

She dried her hands on the rough tea towel that featured chickens and other farm animals. Funny. "Sorry," she whispered to the chickens, so quietly that nobody heard her.

"Thank you for coming," her mom said as she walked them to the door. It sounded so strange, so formal. Like she'd just made an obligatory social call to a long-lost relative.

"It was good seeing you," Poppy said. Her mom grabbed her and hugged her tight. She felt Ryan's presence beside her. When she tried to let go, her mom held tighter for just a moment. Finally, Poppy relaxed a bit into her.

"Thanks for bringing her," her mom said to Ryan, though she barely looked at him.

"Oh, I didn't—I mean, thank you for lunch. It was great," he said. *Great? Since when do you not eat?*

"You have a safe drive back," her mom told her. She reached up as if she was going to smooth Poppy's hair, but stopped and pulled her hand back.

"We will," Poppy said.

"You take care of my baby," her mom said as she turned to Ryan. Poppy shifted from side to side. Her mom had never been so overtly protective before, and especially not like this. She had to admit, a part of her was comforted by it.

"I will," Ryan said without hesitation. Poppy looked at him curiously. *You will?*

"Okay. Bye, you two," her mom said, and closed the door behind them. The click of the lock bid them farewell.

As Poppy descended the gray steps, Ryan took her elbow and guided her along the short gravel driveway. "You okay?" he asked.

She could only nod, and kept her head turned away from him. He couldn't see her like this. Although she willed the tears away, a single drop fell as she reached the car. Poppy let her hair fall over her face as Ryan walked to the passenger side.

Why did her parents still have this much power over her? She never expected the visits to be easy, but when they were this hard that couldn't be normal. Could it? Didn't other people her age visit their parents, have a good time, and leave happy?

As Poppy slid into the driver seat and turned the ignition, she took one final look at the falling-apart house her mother spent day after day in. What kind of life was that? The lawn was crying out for help, the weeds out of control, and black-berry bushes crept across the property lines.

Soon, the entire place would be overtaken. Given back to the wild. Perhaps that's just how it was supposed to be.

14

***

RYAN

*H*e'd watched her hold it together for the past few hours. The tension in the car had been bottled up so tight by the time they'd arrived at her parents' house it was palpable. He'd thought the lunch would be awkward, and it certainly was. There was even a part of him that had felt tricked into going. But once he saw how bad it was, and how much Poppy needed someone, all his wariness had faded away.

He wasn't surprised at all when she pulled over a few blocks from the house and started bawling. In fact, he didn't know how she'd managed to hold it together as long as she had.

"Hey, hey, it's alright," he said as he unbuckled both their seat belts and pulled her toward him. She was silent, but shook vigorously. He felt her warm tears as they spilled onto his neck.

She was limp as a ragdoll, and he easily boosted her closer. Poppy was awkwardly half on his lap. He squeezed and released her shoulder, uncertain of what to say or do. He'd seen her family "situation" before firsthand of course, but that was different. Back then, he'd had adrenaline to tell him what to do. But now? It was just the two of them, and all he wanted was to take her pain away.

As her tremors stilled, she lifted herself from his chest and wiped the tears away. "Sorry," she whispered. Their eyes met, and even through the glassy tearstained gaze, he saw that same look she'd had the other day by the pool. It was a considering look. And this time he couldn't resist.

It was like a stranger was directing him. He leaned forward and closed the distance between them. When his lips met hers, a jolt shot through him like he'd never felt before. She responded hungrily. As if she'd been starving so many years.

She tasted unbelievably sweet, in a way he would never have imagined. Yet the saltiness of her tears also coated her lips and had snuck into her mouth. The taste, her taste, blended into an intricate medley that was addictive.

Ryan flicked his tongue across her teeth, and she parted her lips wider, receptive. When their tongues met, he tasted another layer of her flavors and couldn't get enough. She was the sweetest thing his lips, his tongue, had ever known.

Poppy let out a gentle moan, her chest pushed firmly against his, and he was instantly hard. It felt good, way too right. *Fuck.*

Suddenly, Poppy pulled away. Embarrassed, she backed away to the driver side. "Ow," she said as the stick shift dug into her thigh.

Ryan opened his mouth to say something, he wasn't sure what. But Poppy beat him to it. "I'm sorry," she said. "That was… that wasn't right."

Sorry? Wasn't right? Didn't she feel the same thing he did?

"Poppy, I—"

"No," she said as she held up a hand. "That was… wow. Okay. A moment of weakness? I guess? That sounds really lame, but I don't know what else to call it."

"You think I took advantage of you?" he asked. Maybe he had. Maybe he'd misread the whole thing. The last few days, the pool, everything.

"No, I don't mean that," she said. Her face softened with the slightest of smiles. "I mean, it was both of us. We both… what about Will?"

"Will?" Hell, he'd forgotten all about him.

"Yeah, my boyfriend?" The defensiveness crept steadily into her voice.

"What about him?" He could never resist a challenge.

"Ryan! I'm not the… I can't… you know."

"Do you know?" he asked.

She was quiet and clutched the steering wheel so tight her knuckles were going white. "I don't know what I don't know," she said finally.

"Deep, Poppy."

It felt like she sat there, death grip on the steering wheel, for an hour—though it was probably just one minute, maximum. Finally, without a word, she turned on the ignition and drove onto the main road.

Ryan couldn't believe it. Poppy had pulled the silent treatment on him a few times before, but it was never like this.

Usually it was over a stupid argument they both knew would blow over soon.

This was different. He stole looks at her the entire drive back into the city, but it seemed like she never noticed.

He couldn't bring himself to speak first. *You're a fucking idiot,* he told himself. But he didn't regret it. The way she felt and tasted—she was like a drug.

An hour in a car can feel like days with that kind of tension between two people. And the heat? The passion that tied them together? He wasn't possibly imagining that, was he?

Ryan came up with a thousand different things to say, but none of them made it out of his mouth. *I'm sorry. Didn't you think it felt right? Who gives a damn about Will? I love you.*

Of course he loved her, that wasn't a secret. He couldn't remember if he'd ever actually told her, but it was an unspoken truth between them. But he'd loved her like a friend all those years. Right? He couldn't—he didn't really love her like that, did he?

This is too much. It was a kiss. One kiss! It's shocking it hasn't happened before. How are you this messed up over one kiss?

Still, he couldn't help it. In between thinking of words to break the dual silent treatment, he just kept replaying that kiss over and over in his head.

The single glance he'd taken when his mouth was on hers, he'd seen how beautiful and vulnerable she'd been with her eyes closed millimeters from him. How she tipped her face up and they moved in perfect synchronization, as if this were a dance they'd done their whole lives.

And their lips. How their lips fit together perfectly, the way her bottom lip naturally eased between his lips and his teeth. It was like her mouth had come home.

He could still taste the sweet tea she'd sipped at that afternoon on the tip of her tongue. The heat of her mouth somehow bested his, and it was like sliding into a warm bed that felt just right.

This is ridiculous. It's Poppy!

It had taken all his willpower to stop his hands from roaming. He'd already wrapped her up partially in his lap, but when their lips met he was hyperaware of her thigh draped across his. One hand on her back, the other around her shoulder—thank God he'd had enough self-control to not let his hands roam freely.

He'd barely noticed the flippy little chiffon dress she'd been wearing on the drive to Maryland and during lunch, but in the car? When she was pressed up against him and it was hiked up with all that creamy skin showing? All it would have taken was the slightest of movements and he could have felt that smooth skin all the way up.

It drove him crazy, all the way back to the city. *Did I miss my chance?* All he thought about was how the rest of her must feel. *She couldn't possibly be as good as she felt. Right?*

For the first time, he wondered what she had on underneath all those little dresses and skirts. Sure, she complained about the work clothes all the time, and the few times he'd seen her after a shift she was in jeans, but he knew the real Poppy.

He knew the girl who complained about pants all throughout high school because they were too restricting. He knew the girl who loved spring break in college because she got to wear nothing but swimsuits and pastel sarongs. He knew the girl who went to even eight o'clock pre-med classes in college dressed in denim jackets and long, festival-ready skirts.

How had he never noticed her like that before? And if Poppy tasted even a sliver as good as her lips did, if what she had on under those frilly dresses was even a touch as intriguing as those flirty little skirts… Ryan knew he was in trouble.

The car came to an abrupt halt. He looked at her, but she kept her eyes directly ahead, her foot pressed on the brake. She wasn't even going to put it in park or look at him. They were in front of his building, and this was his last chance. He looked at her, hard, but she wasn't going to give in.

Ryan sighed, turned around and grabbed his messenger bag from the back seat. He opened his mouth to say something to her, anything, but was at a loss.

Just kiss her again. Right now. Take her upstairs and see if what you suspect is true.

The shape of her lips in profile mesmerized him. He could tell her heart rate was up just by her quick rapid breaths. But this was one showdown she was hellbent on not losing.

He wasn't going to be the first to give in. Not now. He held his silence as he stepped out of the car, and barely shut the door before she sped away.

Ryan watched the car retreat down the street. He felt himself grow hard again just thinking about her. Was this what he'd been waiting for? There was something about Poppy he felt like he'd just discovered. Now that he'd had one taste, he needed another. It was like his body demanded it.

But they couldn't… could they?

15

POPPY

The burrito tasted like rubber, but Poppy didn't care. She chewed through the cafeteria lunch special mindlessly. It had been two days since that moment with Ryan, and she hadn't stopped thinking about it. She'd tried, but she just couldn't imagine it was anything less than what it was—sheer magic, heat and passion.

She'd never felt anything like it. Not with Will, not with anybody. And the best part? She hadn't seen it coming, and it had been pure fireworks.

Poppy had replayed it a hundred times, and each time it still made her wet. She imagined how it had felt being cradled on Ryan's lap, the roughness of his jeans against her skin. The thong she wore under her dress covered almost nothing, and even as she'd been crying she was aware of the heat that radiated from him spreading across her thighs and ass.

When he'd moved in and kissed her, it was like that was what she'd been waiting for her entire life. The slight roughness of his stubble brushed her chin and cheeks, and it was a shocking contrast to the suppleness of his lips. When he'd caught her lower lip between his teeth and nibbled slightly, she'd heard a longing moan. It had taken her a moment to realize it came from her. It was like Will didn't even exist and Ryan was her whole world.

His tongue tangled with hers was unlike anything she'd experienced. It felt right, natural, and she'd felt her nipples harden. She couldn't help it. She pushed her breasts against his chest, and that alone had made her flood between her legs.

When she pushed off him, she knew she'd cut the magic short. But she was embarrassed, too humiliated to look down and see if she'd left any of her wetness on his jeans. Instead, she'd acted like a child. Had refused to say a single word to him after her stammered excuses.

She shook her head and let the burrito drop. *You're an idiot.*

She'd wanted to do more than kiss. A lot more. She'd been ready, right then, to give her virginity to Ryan. Actually, it felt like she had been earmarked for him forever.

You stopped right in time, she told herself. *Don't be stupid. You stopped in time... just not early enough to prevent the kiss altogether.*

Well. There was no putting that screeching cat back into the bag now, was there? Poppy groaned and rested her head on her arms, folded across the cafeteria table. *Was that just a one-time thing? Or...*

"What's wrong with you?" Penny flopped down across from Poppy with her own tray of suspicious-looking "Mexican Monday" fare.

"Nothing," Poppy said as she lifted her head to fake normalcy. "Just tired."

"I hear that," Penny said. "I think I got three hours of sleep last night, max."

"Yeah."

"You get any rest?" Penny asked as she took a bite of taco salad and made a face. "Gross, this isn't sour cream."

"I guess."

Penny put down her fork. "Seriously, what's wrong with you? Everything okay?"

Poppy sighed. "I guess I'm having some trouble with Will… or, to put it better, trouble with the lack of him."

Penny smiled knowingly and reached over to pat her shoulder. "It must be hard. Him being gone like this."

How does she know he's gone? Poppy was suddenly on high alert. "I didn't tell you he was gone."

"No?" Penny asked and stuffed another forkful in her mouth. "Hmm. You must have mentioned it at some point."

"I don't remember saying anything."

Poppy shrugged, "Maybe I saw it on Facebook or Twitter then or something."

"Maybe." Poppy rarely posted to social media. She found it too taxing to keep up with. Liking all those posts, retweeting or subtweeting or whatever.

"Anyway, I was just saying, having your boyfriend on the other side of the country can't be any fun," Penny said. "Maybe we should plan a girls' night or something."

The thought of dressing up and hitting the bars with Penny made her roll her eyes. "Ugh, I can't even think about anything but work and sleep right now." *And Ryan.*

"Yeah, I know what you mean. Going out always sounds like a good idea at noon, but by the time six o'clock rolls around I just want to climb into bed with a bottle of wine and watch *The Bachelorette.*"

Poppy smiled. It had been a long time since she'd indulged in one of her vapid, guilty pleasures. "Now that sounds more like it."

"Let me know if you want to do it together sometime this week," Penny said. "I have a date coming up. Maybe you could give me some advice, help me pick out what to wear."

"A date? Who with?" Penny rarely shared details of her love life, and it was a welcome distraction from being stressed over Ryan.

"Oh, uh, just this guy."

"Well, I assumed that."

"Hey now, don't think you know me so well," Penny said. She shook her fork toward Poppy playfully. "For all you know, I might swing both ways."

"Right. You totally strike me as the president of the Ruby Rose fan club." Poppy rolled her eyes. Penny was the straightest girl she'd ever known.

"Hey now! I happen to think women are totally beautiful. I'm more openminded than you think. Shane, from *The L Word?* I'd totally go lesbian for her."

Poppy groaned. "Shush!" she said. "First of all, just because women are beautiful doesn't mean you want to sleep with them. Second of all, anybody would hook up with Shane. And third, I can't believe you just said 'go lesbian.' You're about to get your butt kicked for that total lack of PCness."

Penny giggled. "It's just the two of us, right? I can't censor myself all the time. Besides, I can just blame lack of sleep for my complete lack of sensitivity."

"Yeah," Poppy said. "Speaking of, we just had the sensitivity training seminar last week. Looks like it did you a lot of good." She winked at Penny. It was this kind of giddy mindlessness that made her want to be friends with the crazy girl in the first place. When they got into their rhythm, it made the shifts fly by.

"So, back to the important stuff... I'm serious. Were you talking about Ryan?" Penny's eyes were big as she shoved carnitas in her mouth.

"No! Penny, honestly... it's just that Will's still in LA." She forced a laugh and said, "He's been gone so long other men are starting to distract me!"

Poppy said it like it was a joke, but Penny's eyes narrowed. "You mean Ryan."

"Please," Poppy said as she rolled her eyes. *Don't be stupid, you're saying way too much.* Penny was smarter than she acted.

"Poppy," Penny said. She reached across the table again and grabbed Poppy's arm. "Are you holding out on me?"

"I didn't mean anything by it! I was joking, forget I said anything." She knew it would look suspicious, but she jumped up from the table and grabbed her tray. "I should be getting back," she said. *Shut up! Penny knows your schedule.*

She dumped the flavorless burrito in the compost bin and fished her keys out of her jacket. Forget changing, she'd do it at home.

Penny was acting weird, for sure, she thought as she pulled out of the parking lot. Did Penny just disapprove, or was it more than that?

They weren't really close, but there was a natural camaraderie that unfolded when you shared shift rounds with someone. Normally, Poppy would have been happy to have someone to dismantle this mess with. Now, it felt like all her usual confidantes were tangled up in the same web with her. Ryan, Will, Penny, the whole lot. Even Sarah. *Oh, wow, I forgot about Sarah in all this.* Sarah would kill her.

You're in a mess. A real big, sloppy mess. As she pulled up to where the road forked in three directions, she gave a wry smile. *Fitting. I'm literally at a fork in the road.*

It was time to decide. For her, down one path was the future she'd always thought she'd have. Will would be a decent husband, and there would surely be kids and that white picket fence—or at least a brick privacy fence. It was safe, secure, and she knew what to expect. Maybe their kids would even inherit some of his creativity. Lord knows she didn't have any.

And down that other path? She didn't know. It was full of the promise of excitement, seasoned with plenty of uncertainty. Until now, she hadn't even known that path existed. It was wild and not well traveled. What did they call those kinds of trails again? *Desire paths. That's right. The trails blazed from pure desire—even while there are other trails that are obviously marked and cleared.*

Will was at the end of one path, and Ryan the other. Well, maybe. Down Will's path, it was all concrete but the plans were clear. Ryan's path was full of potential turmoil. She might lose her best friend. Ryan's path might not even be an option; it might all be a figment of her imagination.

The car behind her honked, and she noticed the light was green.

As she lifted her foot off the brake, she didn't know if she'd be turning right or left. She always turned right here, since it took her home. However, as Robert Frost's poem began to recite in her head, dug up from her undergraduate Literary Criticism class, she chose left.

Let's just see where it goes.

16

RYAN

"Ryan, I haven't seen you since BUD/S, man." Ryan slapped Li on the back, and shook hands with Garret. "What you been up to? Besides sipping on those green drinks?" Li nodded to the extra-large protein smoothie in Ryan's hand.

"Not much," Ryan said. "I was just discharged not that long ago. Knee," he said, and nodded to his leg. "You both still active duty?"

"Nah," replied Li. "Went into the Marshals. We both did," he said, and nodded at Garret.

"No shit, that's what I've been looking into. The recruiter left me a message yesterday, actually. Seems like they have some kind of fast-track, on-the-job training option."

"You should do it!" Garret said. He squinted his sky blue eyes and adjusted his hat brim.

"Yeah? You like it?"

"It's awesome," Garret said. "Good pay, and you can pretty much cherry-pick your details and location."

"Yeah," Li said. "If you're military, especially SEAL, you're golden."

"What have they had you doing?"

Li shrugged. "Actually, we work together," he said. "Mostly taking care of vehicles seized from criminals. It's a lot of paperwork, but you get to handle some pretty sweet rides."

"Last week it was a Bugatti Chiron," Garret said. "The whole back end was kitted out to transport blow. And, what, six weeks ago? We actually got a Koenigsegg Regera processed. Unbelievable, I never thought I'd see one of those, let alone drive it."

"They let you drive it?" Ryan asked, impressed.

"Well, from the pickup site to the processing center. Just a few miles, but it was incredible."

"Sounds great, man," Ryan said. Moving around million-dollar cars wasn't his idea of a dream job, but he saw the appeal. Exotic rides were all Li and Garret had talked about in training.

"You should do it, give 'em a call back," Li said. "Actually, who're you talking to? Lieutenant Dan?"

"Stevens," Ryan said.

"Yeah man, that's him. Don't he look like Lieutenant Dan, though? That's what we call him."

"Who the hell is Lieutenant Dan?"

"Man, didn't you ever see *Forrest Gump*? Anyway, yeah, it's the same guy. I can call in an informal rec if you want."

Ryan sized up Li. For all his arrogance and preening, he'd kept a flawless record in the SEALs. Maybe running into him and Garret on the street was a sign. What could it hurt?

"Yeah, sure, why not?" he said.

"Cool. I'll call him in a few. I'll let him know you'll call him this afternoon?"

Ryan felt the pressure already start to build. Li had always moved fast, but seemed so laidback nobody saw it coming.

"Uh, yeah. Will do."

"Alright, cool. See you later, brother." Li went in for one of his complicated handshake-fist bump combinations, and Ryan was surprised to see he remembered it even after all these years.

"*L*ieutenant Stevens." Ryan clutched his phone. *Why are you nervous?*

"Lieutenant, this is PO Scott," he said.

"Scott. Yeah, PO Li said you'd be calling. What can I do for you? I'm assuming you got my message yesterday."

"Yes, sir. I'm curious where you have work available. For the on-the-job fast-track."

"Pretty much everywhere," the lieutenant said with a laugh. "Like I said, US Marshals aren't suffering from an overabundance of qualified applicants."

"What about locally?"

"Locally, nationwide, anywhere. You can fill out the paperwork today if you'd like, it's all online. A lot of new hires start out with small projects locally, then build up to more national positions—or even international."

"That sounds perfect, sir. Thank you. I'll fill out the forms now."

"Good, son. Just click on the link in the initial email from a few weeks ago. It has the PIN and everything you need. The only thing I'll need from you in person is biometric data and a few ink signatures. Can you come in this week?"

"Yes, sir. Whatever day and time works for you."

"I'll send you a calendar invitation in a few minutes. Isn't technology something?"

Ryan smiled. "Yes, sir."

He hung up and rubbed the back of his neck. *What now?* His mind wandered to Poppy, the way she'd looked in that parking lot when she was half seated on his lap. The warmth of her mouth. *Stop it,* he told himself, and pushed her out of his mind.

That was crazy, the other day. Kissing her like that. He stood on the precipice of lighting a lifetime of friendship on fire. Not just friendship, the best friendship he'd ever had. By a long shot. He couldn't figure out why he'd never seen how perfect she was—not just on the inside. That was something he'd always known. But on the outside, too.

In high school, he'd lucked onto the varsity football team as a sophomore. He was just a running back, but the coach had seen his potential and wanted to groom him with the star players. By his junior year he was the quarterback, which pissed Evan off something fierce. Evan was the senior who'd been most likely to earn the position, and when the coach gave it to Ryan tension on the team mounted.

"Yo, Ryan," Evan had said after one of the first practices of the season. He'd cornered him in the locker room. None of the other guys dared to look up. "What's up with you and that Poppy girl?"

Poppy? Ryan had been expecting some shit about the practice. Maybe even a little scuffle. Evan's approach threw him off guard.

"Poppy? Not much," Ryan said. Poppy had managed the first half of high school going largely unnoticed. She had her own little group of friends, a hodgepodge collection of girls who didn't really fit into any cliques.

"C'mon, that's not what I heard," Evan said. He pulled either end of the towel that hung around his neck, and flexed so Ryan could see just how much bigger the senior was.

"Don't know what you heard," Ryan said as he pulled on his jeans. No matter how often he changed in the locker room, there was always a feeling of vulnerability.

"I heard you were fucking her six ways from Sunday," Evan said. Ryan's ears went red. "Not that I blame you, dude! That's a hot piece of ass right there. Doesn't say much, sure. But the quiet ones are always the freaks in bed. Ain't I right?"

Fucking her? Even as he went into his junior year, Ryan was still getting used to the enormous social pressure to engage in locker room talk—but he just couldn't. He had to stick to the truth, especially when it came to Poppy.

"It's not like that," Ryan said as he buckled his fly.

"Oh yeah? I guess not. Not with you at least. Me? If I was up near that good-good like you, she wouldn't be walking straight for a week."

Ryan had clenched his fist to still the full-body shaking. The last thing he needed was a fight with Evan, but he couldn't let him talk about Poppy like that.

"Good luck with that." It was all he could manage. Luckily, Evan just laughed and walked away.

Most of high school was like that, and Ryan never understood. Evan wasn't the first on the team to ask him about Poppy. For Ryan, it was a badge of honor just to have a female friend. And yeah, as it turned out, Evan was right. A really hot female friend.

*H*e pinched his nose and logged into his tablet to fill out the forms. He really couldn't afford to think about Poppy, not like that.

As he started to fill in the information, his phone buzzed.

Hey, stranger. Drinks later? Sarah. She'd been slipping from his mind more and more. He watched the ellipses roll across his phone. *Live game show at Three Sheets tonight. Prob stupid fun.*

A game show. That was exactly what he needed. He used to race back to his place with Poppy after school to suck down Otter Pops and binge on *Supermarket Sweep. Sure, see you there*, he replied.

He didn't feel much for Sarah, but didn't feel badly about it, either. It felt like the casual thing between them was mutual. Besides, that could change. Couldn't it? She was a nice girl, a pretty girl. Maybe something would grow between them. Everyone always talked about taking it slow, but nobody did. What was wrong with avoiding a crash and burn?

Sarah was growing on him, too. Slowly. He'd found out she wasn't so much annoying as blessed with a strange sense of humor. Plus, few things really bothered her. She was the ultimate low-key, go with the flow type of girl.

Ryan undressed, dropped his clothes to the floor in the bathroom, and turned on the shower water as hot as it would go. As the water fell over him, he couldn't stop thinking about Poppy. His cock hardened, and he willed himself to think about Sarah instead. But he couldn't even remember her face.

Screw it. He gripped his cock at the base and squeezed gently. Images of Poppy flashed in his mind. He pictured her in that skimpy white bikini by the pool—but this time, it was just the two of them.

"Do me now," she said, and flipped onto her stomach. Ryan's hand worked up his shaft to the tip as he remembered how her skin had felt against his. Soft, warm and buttery smooth.

But this time, he didn't have to be careful. He rubbed his hands over her shoulders, down her shoulder blades and untied the back of her bikini with a single pull. His hands brushed against the fullness of the sides of her breasts, and the curves of her body demanded he move quickly to her small waist. He grabbed the bar of soap to slicken his hand, and began to stroke himself faster.

Her bikini bottoms were tied neatly with a bow on either side, a present to unwrap. He tore into her like a kid at Christmas, untying both sides simultaneously. When he whipped the bottoms off of her, pulled them with one hand from beneath her, she looked over her shoulder and smiled. But still, she didn't turn over. And he couldn't make out the details of her face. Besides that smile, she could be anyone.

Ryan clutched her ass cheeks and spread them apart with his thumb. Slightly, she lifted her hips and gave him a better view. From her perfect, pink rosebud to her swollen lips, juicy entry and engorged clit, the entirety of her was incredible. "Do me now," she said again.

He moved into the rhythm he knew would make him come soon. Even in his fantasy, he didn't want anything to happen too fast. He wanted to take his time and explore every part of her.

With one hand, he slid his fingers between her legs and toyed with her lips. Already, they were slick with her wetness. He moved a finger between her folds and flicked lightly at her clit. She shuddered and raised her hips higher, her body begging for him.

As he continued to play with her clit, she started to move against his hand. His balls began to tighten as he imagined slipping one finger into her while his thumb circled the rim of her ass. Even just imagining her tightness and wetness was enough to make him come.

He steadied himself against the wall in the shower and thought about the roundness of her ass cheeks as she rode his hand and came hard, drenching him all the way to the wrist.

Ryan groaned and closed his eyes. He had an hour before he was meeting Sarah, but was still watching the last of his come spiral down the drain.

1 7

RYAN

FOURTEEN YEARS AGO

*R*yan took a deep breath and knocked on Poppy's door. The rented tuxedo felt strange and itchy. He couldn't help but wonder how many boys had worn it before—boys going to their first prom, or even men on their wedding day. He'd never been the school dance type, but Poppy had begged him to take her. He never could tell her no.

Besides, they were just juniors. It wasn't their real senior prom anyway. He'd done his research and found out his cummerbund was supposed to match her dress. Ryan never thought he'd be wearing pink silk, but here he was. In his hands, he clutched a plastic box holding a pink poppy corsage. The florist had told him a bright pink would contrast nicely with her light pink dress.

He hoped the flower wouldn't wilt until after the photos at least. "Ryan!" Poppy's mom said. "What are you…"

"Hi, Mrs. Baker. Is Poppy ready?"

"Poppy? Well, yes, but…"

Her mom trailed off and opened the door wider. Inside, Poppy had a digital camera held overhead as she snapped a selfie with a guy he'd never seen before. Even in that small moment, he could tell the guy was from the prep school across town. It was in how he held himself; the high quality of the tuxedo was evident even from the doorway. *Since when did Poppy hang out with guys like that? Or guys at all?*

His own rented tuxedo suddenly felt unbearably cheap. It didn't matter that for him, it had cost nearly a month's salary. Working part-time wasn't that big of a deal in their school. There were a lot of kids who worked. Some because they had to, like him, and some because they wanted the extra cash to upgrade the sound system in their secondhand cars.

Poppy didn't see him, but he caught sight of Mr. Baker. The man beamed as he took the camera from Poppy and started directing them like he was making the music video of the year. "Put your hands on her waist. That's it," he said. The guy with the jet black, perfectly combed hair gripped Poppy's waist dutifully.

She looked miserable, but she complied. "Smile!" her father said loudly, and she plastered a fake grin on her face. Poppy looked suddenly to the door, as if Ryan had called her. Since they'd met, they'd shared an uncanny ability to communicate without words.

He opened his mouth, but she shook her head sternly and bit her lip. In her eyes was a sorrowful apology. "Poppy! Pay attention," her father snapped, and her gaze shifted back to the camera.

"I'm sorry, Ryan," her mom said.

"Colleen, shut the goddamned door!" her father yelled. Mrs. Baker sadly shut the door and murmured apologies the entire time.

Shocked, Ryan descended the stairs and pulled the bow tie off his neck. Eli had helped him tie it after consulting a how-to video, and it had taken fifteen minutes. He undid the work in just a few seconds. *What the hell do I do now?*

He began to wander and saw Poppy's neighborhood with fresh eyes. For all the times they'd ran and biked up and down these streets, he'd never really noticed them. The cracked sidewalks, the indoor furniture shoved onto so many front porches, and the piles of motorcycles on some of the lawns were all reminders of where they came from.

Funny how you can spend most of your childhood and youth not really knowing that you're poor—until some rich kid from across town shows you without saying anything.

He heaved himself onto their special bench at Mitchell Park. Ryan hadn't even realized that's where he was going, but it made sense. The sunset was a romantic one, and he took in the blaze of colors on his own. *How many classmates are watching this same scene, with their date pressed into their arms?* Eventually, the purples and pinks gave way to blackness. Stars peeked through the veil of darkness. He hadn't a clue what time it was.

He felt her presence before he saw her. Quietly, Poppy sat down beside him. "I didn't want to go with Lawrence," she said.

Lawrence? Was that really his name? Ryan bubbled over with so much anger, he couldn't bring himself to speak.

"Ryan, I'm really sorry," she said. "He's—he's my dad's boss' son. He's seen pictures of me at work. Weird, right? That my dad would have a picture of any of us there? And he asked to take me."

Ryan sniffed and looked at his hands, cupped in his lap. *You couldn't say no?*

"I didn't have a choice, I couldn't say no," she said. He glanced up, but not at her. Could she really read his mind? "Ryan, please."

He sighed. When she pleaded like that, she could break through him with ease. "How was prom?" he asked.

"Terrible. I mean, of course it was terrible. Cheesy streamers and balloons for decorations. The food sucked, you would have hated that."

He laughed. "And what about your fancy-pants date?"

"Oh, wow," she said. "Bad. Really bad. Apparently that whole eighties 'prom is for sex' stereotype is still lodged deeply in that jerk's mind. He kept asking the whole time if I wanted to 'go under the bleachers.'"

"So, did you?" Ryan asked with a smile. Even though he knew it was ridiculous, he wanted Poppy's reassurance.

"No! Don't be weird," she said. "I told him he could go by himself. Then he said he had a hotel room downtown at the Ritz with strawberries and champagne waiting."

"Are you serious?"

"Yeah, and all I could think of was Julia Roberts in *Pretty Woman.* I told him I didn't have the boots or blonde wig for that."

He laughed again. "I think you could totally pull off thigh-high boots and a hooker wig."

She elbowed him in the ribs. "That's why I'm back so early," she said. "I know I was talking about this stupid dance forever, but…"

"But what? Are you okay? Did something else happen?"

She smiled grimly. "I took care of it myself. Besides, what I was saying was… it wasn't the dance. It was going with you. With my best friend. I'm sorry, Ry. I messed up."

He lifted his arm and she slid against his chest with ease. As she rested her head on his shoulder, he wrapped his hand around her bare upper arm. "I'm sorry your night was so bad," he said. "Both our nights could use a do-over."

"It's not so bad now," she said, and looked up at him with a glint in her eyes.

"Cheesy," he said.

"It's prom. It's supposed to be cheesy."

"What time is it?" he asked her.

"You never wear a watch. Not even eleven," she said as she looked at her slim golden watch. It was her mother's, reserved for fancy occasions.

"It's technically still prom night then. Here," he said, and handed her the pink poppy. Miraculously, it still looked fresh.

"Oh, Ryan," she said, a little sadly. "I really am sorry."

He helped her put it on her wrist. "It's okay," he said. A dark car in the parking lot across the street turned alive with music. They both looked at it. There must have been kids making out and hooking up in the back seat the whole time he was here. He laughed. "Kids," he said.

The car's radio shifted into Shaggy's "Angel."

"Well," Ryan said as he stood up. "Should we dance? Sorry, there aren't any bleachers around here to invite you to."

She rolled her eyes as he helped her up. "This is like, straight cheesy," she said. "You didn't plan this, did you?"

"Oh yeah," Ryan said as he took her in his arms. "It was all part of my master plan to spend the night out in the park alone with a pink flower while I synchronized with the Honda in the parking lot for your arrival."

Poppy laughed. "I'm sure," she said. "But seriously, this is so much better than the real prom. And I'm sorry. Truly."

"It's not your fault," Ryan said. He could feel the heat from her back through the slippery satin. She radiated it.

"That doesn't make it okay," she said. She rested her head on his shoulder.

"A lot of things aren't okay. But this? This is pretty good. And at least this tux and horrible shoes get to show off a little bit."

"Yeah, those are pretty ugly shoes," she said.

"Hey! The guy at the shop said these were dope. Those were his exact words."

She lifted her head and looked at him. "Ryan, if a salesman tells you something is dope, you probably shouldn't get it."

He shrugged. "Lesson learned. But how many other guys are dancing under the moonlight with a girl who ditched her date for them tonight?"

She slapped him playfully on the chest. "Probably only you."

"See?" he asked as he twirled her in a circle. "The shoes work."

18

―――――――

POPPY

"This place is insane," she told Sarah. They both shifted in the uncomfortable wooden seats, arranged in a semicircle around the dance floor that had been turned into a game show stage for the night.

"I know, right? And on a Thursday." Sarah took small sips from her beer.

"There's Ryan!" Poppy said. She lifted an arm to wave him over. The surprised look on his face told her he hadn't known she was coming. "Didn't you tell him I was coming?" she asked Sarah as Ryan weaved his way through the crowd.

"I figured he'd assume," Sarah said. She picked her bag up from the seat between them for Ryan to sit.

"I'm the peanut butter in a lady sandwich, huh?" Ryan asked as he sat down. Poppy offered up a smile, but it was forced. "Anyone else coming?"

"Nope, it's a threesome tonight," Sarah said with a wink. "Consider yourself lucky."

"I always do," Ryan said. He grabbed a handful of Poppy's popcorn without asking, and she automatically angled the paper bag in his direction.

"Alright folks, it's time to get started!" The emcee was a balding man with a paunch. "Now, as some of you know, this is a traveling show every Thursday night at various hot spots around town. To keep things interesting, every week it's a new game, and we try to keep the details on the down low. You know what I'm saying?"

A few drunk people in the audience whooped and hollered.

"That's right! Tonight's game is all about how well do you know your partner?"

Poppy felt awkward as blood rushed to her face. *Obviously you're the odd man out. Or woman.* Oh well, at least it would be entertaining and she wouldn't have to worry about getting called up on stage.

Sarah gave her an apologetic look. "Sorry," she said. "I didn't know—"

"It's okay," Poppy said.

"We probably won't get picked anyway. But if we do, we'll all go up. Pinky swear," she said, and held up a symbolic pinky.

"Do you two want to sit together?" Ryan asked as he munched through more of the popcorn. He didn't take his eyes off the stage.

"You just be happy sitting bitch," Sarah told him with a poke to his arm.

"Ouch! Watch those talons," Ryan said.

The emcee chose some easy prey in the first row—two couples who were clearly in the honeymoon stages of their relationship. The first couple "passed" with flying colors, which moved them to the semifinal rounds. The second couple admitted they were just on their third date. They were clearly nervous, and Poppy thought it was cute. She began to relax into the fun of the evening.

She nursed her cocktail and stole glances at her watch. The whole thing was entertaining enough, but she couldn't shake the idea she was crashing Ryan and Sarah's date.

"And, I'm sorry, but with that answer you're disqualified," the emcee said. Poppy looked up, and the newish couple stood up to exit. "She answered that her idea of a perfect vacation is somewhere tropical, not a snow-covered mountain lodge." The couple in the semifinal rounds smiled confidently from their corner.

Is it too early to call it a night? Poppy downed the last of her drink and started to wriggle on her jacket.

"Now, how about… you!" the emcee said.

"Me?" Ryan was caught with a fistful of popcorn halfway to his mouth.

"Yes, the handsome, muscular man in the middle there. Which one of those pretty girls are you here with?"

"Well, both—"

"Both! Lucky dog!"

"No, I mean, uh. She—she's my date," Ryan stammered as he put a hand on Sarah's shoulder.

"Well, bring her on down!"

"Poppy! Poppy, come on," Sarah said. She grabbed Poppy's arm and dragged her up.

"No! Sarah, you go—"

"Come on! I told you we were doing this all together."

Afraid to make a scene, Poppy let Sarah herd her to the stage.

"Oh, I see it is a threesome after all! That's okay, let's roll with this," the emcee said. He gestured for an assistant to bring out an extra chair and situated the three of them on stage.

"What's your name?" he asked.

"Poppy."

"And your friend here?"

"Uh, Sarah."

"Uh Sarah. Got it. Okay, I'm going to ask you some questions about your friend first to get things rolling."

As he tore through the questions, she got one after the other correct. They were easy, especially since she and Sarah had lived together briefly in college.

"Favorite hangover food? Worst date? Drink of choice?" *This is easier than I thought.*

"Now, Sarah," the host said. "I'm going to ask you some questions about Ryan. That is, assuming you know anything about him besides how good he looks in a T-shirt."

Poppy saw Sarah tense up. Even though the emcee was joking, it was a sore spot for Sarah. She was notorious for "
not being able to keep a man."

"Okay," Sarah said, her tone determined.

"What's his favorite hobby?"

"Eating." Ryan laughed and nodded.

"Your first kiss?"

Poppy hummed in her head. She didn't want to hear the answer, but saw Ryan nod again.

"Where was he born?"

"Virginia."

Ryan shook his head. "Oh, that looks like a no! Ryan?" the emcee asked.

"Oregon. Long story, nobody knows that," Ryan said apologetically. *I knew that,* Poppy thought. His mom had been traveling for work during her third trimester and Ryan had arrived early, a surprise preemie.

Poppy began willing Sarah to get the rest of the answers right, and she did pretty well. In all, she answered sixteen of the nineteen questions correctly.

"Now, whether this last question is answered correctly or not doesn't really matter," the emcee said. "You're still doing well enough for the semifinals and the chance to win a gift certificate worth over two hundred dollars to this esteemed pub. But let's make things interesting—Poppy? I'm directing the last question to you, and it's about Ryan."

Poppy sat up straight. "But first, do you know if Ryan went to his prom?"

"Yeah. He did," she said.

"Great. What was the name of his prom date? His first prom date, if he went to multiple?"

She could feel Sarah's eyes as they bored into her. "I don't remember her name," Poppy finally said. Sarah glowed, happy that Poppy wasn't so perfect after all. She didn't know Ryan that much better than Sarah did. Or at least it looked that way.

"Sixteen points!" the emcee said, and an assistant pointed them toward the semifinal table.

"I need to go to the restroom," Sarah whispered to them both, flushed with excitement.

"I need another drink," Poppy said, and raced to the bar.

She ordered an ice water, and felt a hand on her arm. "Poppy! What the hell was that?" She turned, and Ryan was right behind her. "How could you? How could you not—"

Poppy looked away, but he wasn't going to give up. At the end of the long bar, they were in a quiet, dark corner with just a neglected jukebox. "Ryan, come on—"

"No," he said. In one step he engulfed her personal space. She felt caged.

"Knock it off, this is stupid—"

She tried to move around him, but she was truly cornered. He pressed his body firmly against hers to keep her in place. The full presence of him chilled her to the bone. A hardness pressed into her hip and her eyes went wide. She'd never really been aware of him like this before, and the pressure of his cock against her shocked her to stillness.

Poppy bit her lip and looked down. *What would he taste like…*

Of course she'd had his lips, and not that long ago. The feel of his tongue working hers was still fresh in her memory. It sprung up at the most inopportune times, like when she was halfway through a shift. Or in the middle of the night when she really needed sleep but couldn't stop the ache between her legs. *But would he taste different? Better, somehow? Down there...*

She wanted him so badly it knocked the breath out of her. *It's like there are two of you, Jekyll and Hyde. Which path are you going to take? Come on, come on, come on.*

There was still a part of her that was hungry for Will's path. At least there, she would have certainty. Follow Ryan's path, and it would be straight down a rabbit hole to a fate unknown. "Ryan—"

"Poppy." Was it her imagination, or was he pressing himself harder into her? The heat and pressure against her hip bone were too much to take.

"I have a boyfriend," she said. Poppy shoved Ryan's chest and forced him to back up. Just like that, the spell was broken.

"I know," he growled.

"Then act like it." She pushed past him and bolted out of the door into the cool sweetness of the night air. *You're an idiot for getting so close. Almost kissing him again.*

She started walking toward her car, parked blocks away. Her phone buzzed at least a dozen times, but she refused to look. It would just be Ryan, apologizing again, and she didn't have any room left for him in her head. Instead, she focused on keeping her heels from getting stuck in the sidewalk cracks and politely telling the homeless men huddled in the doorways she didn't have any cash.

"Liar," one called after her. Maybe he was right.

What is wrong with me? She couldn't be having these feelings, these urges—not about her best friend.

19

RYAN

"Poppy, seriously call me back. I know you're getting these." It was the sixth message he'd left for her in five days. He'd stopped counting how many texts he'd sent. Ever since the incident at the pub, she'd been completely ignoring him. Sarah, however, seemed over the moon—something about that game show had really gotten her hot and bothered, even though they hadn't won.

Fuck it, I'm going over there. Poppy's schedule changed every week, so he wasn't certain when she'd be off work. Her car wasn't parked in its spot, which meant he could ambush her on the stairs when she finally got home.

He grabbed a book out of the trunk, along with a hoodie, and settled on the concrete steps for possibly hours of waiting. "You locked out?" a neighbor asked an hour later. It was an older woman with arms full of groceries.

"No, waiting on my—my sister," he said. It might sound stalkerish if he said anything else.

"The girl in 312?" the woman asked. He stood up and took one of her bags to help her to the door.

"Yeah, Poppy," he said. The woman shook her head. "That girl's never gone."

"Yeah, well. I'll wait," he said. By the time he saw Poppy's car pull up, it was nearly dark and he had to squint to read in the dim stairwell lighting.

She walked up the stairs with heavy, tired steps. When she saw him, her mouth hardened. "Poppy, I'm sorry," he said before she could get a word in.

Poppy looked at him, incredulous. "Sorry won't cut it anymore, Ryan."

"Come on, Poppy—"

"Don't," she said firmly. "Just don't. Being sorry and then doing the same thing over and over again, expecting a different outcome—that's the definition of madness, isn't it?"

"I know, I know," he said. "All I can say is I'm sorry. And hope that you'll forgive me. I don't want all our years of friendship to be erased. They're more important to me than anything else." It was almost impossible to get those last words out. A lump had formed in his throat and threatened to burst.

She eyed him carefully. Calculations raced across her face, and he didn't know how he was being judged. "Alright," she said finally. "You can be forgiven one more time. As long as you say it."

"Say what?" He was totally lost.

"Apologize for what you did, specifically, and I'll be satisfied with that." Her eyes carried a calmness, a coolness, that he'd never seen in her before. He couldn't tell if it was a challenge or a dare, but he would have done anything in that moment.

"I'm sorry that I hit on you again. That shouldn't have happened."

"It shouldn't have happened because…" she prompted.

"Because you have a boyfriend."

"Because we're friends," Poppy said as she rolled her eyes. "Best friends. Not because of some guy, but because you should respect me more than that."

Ryan lowered his head, truly ashamed. She was right. Why was he deferring to that jackass Will? It was about Poppy, about their friendship. He knew that. Ryan felt like a dog with his tail between his legs.

There was a part of him that wanted to argue with her. Make her admit she felt something between them, too—that he wasn't alone in the attraction. But for now at least, he had to push that urge away.

Poppy didn't say anything more, but she didn't break her gaze. She was still deciding something, still unsure. Finally, she gave a slight nod and moved past him.

"Are you coming in?" she asked with a sigh as she unlocked the door.

Ryan followed behind her. "I need to change," she said. "I wasn't up for facing the locker room today." She took her knapsack and went to her bedroom. She pulled the door behind her, but it didn't close completely. There was a tiny crack, not enough to see anything even if he tried, but he couldn't help but stare at it. Did she want him to follow her?

He sat on the couch, torn. Just knowing she had stripped down just a few steps away, that she was probably naked and sifting through her dresser, he got hard instantly. It put him on edge. "My Netflix has been weird," she called from the bedroom. "Maybe you can get it to work, though." Unable to stop, like something deep inside directed him, he leaned back to see if he could spot her.

And there she was. At the right angle, he saw her in violet underwear and no bra, though her back was to him. She'd untied her long blonde hair, and those now-familiar dimples on her lower back—the ones that seemed like they were made for his fingers—teased him as they rode right above the lace fringe of the violet material.

"Or I think I still have my Hulu subscription, if there's something on that," she called as she pulled on silk pajama bottoms and a pink tank top. "Will usually fixes it, but he's stayed longer in LA." With a practiced hand, she pulled her hair back up into a high, messy knot. "He seems to be doing good though. 'Making contacts' and all that. I mean, I'm happy for him, but it feels like the distance isn't really making the heart grow fonder, if you know what I mean."

She'd left the bra off. His cock jumped in his pants. He grabbed a throw pillow and put it over his crotch.

"But you know, I'm sure all that will be fixed when he comes back. Distance is hard," she said.

He couldn't agree more. Ryan pressed down on the cushion, trying to stop his erection in case she wanted him to get up.

"Ry?" she asked. Her head was poked out of the bedroom. "Are you listening?"

He realized he hadn't said a single word since she went in the bedroom. "Yes," he said with a smile.

"Okay. You're being quiet. I want to wash my face; I feel gross after that fourteen-hour shift. Want to order a pizza and find a movie to watch?"

"Yeah, sure. Georgie's okay?" he asked.

"Whatever. You'll be the one eating ninety-five percent of it."

He heard her pad into the bathroom en suite and the water turned on. Ryan looked up the takeout number on his phone and called in the order. "No onions," he said.

"You sure?" the girl asked on the other end. "We have caramelized onions that—"

"I'm sure," he said.

He toyed around with some of the Netflix settings until the error message disappeared. As he flipped through the recommendations, new releases and recently added titles, he was acutely aware of any plots that might be awkward. Romcoms were mostly out. Dramas were probably going to be too depressing. He was way too riled up to deal with subtitles, so that took international films out of the running.

By the time he heard the water stop, he was down to horror and thrillers.

"How long?" she asked as she emerged from the bedroom. Her face glowed. Without any makeup, she looked so young —like they were in high school again.

"Thirty, forty-five minutes," he said.

She made a face. "I'm hungry."

"It's coming."

"Horror?" she asked as she curled up on the other end of the couch. Was that intentional? *Is she trying to keep her distance, or do we always commandeer opposite ends of the couch and I've never noticed?*

"Not in the mood?" he asked.

"It's fine," she said. "You've just never taken a real interest before."

He shrugged. "Things change."

"Yeah," she said, and stole a glance from the corner of her eye. "I guess they do. Just nothing too over the top," she said. "I hate that. Gore for gore's sake. I feel like I get enough of that in the ER rounds."

He'd forgotten about that. About what her day must look like. "How about this?" he asked.

"Oh wow, Ryan. *Visiting Hours*? Seriously?"

"It's got William Shatner in it!"

"The guy from the Priceline commercials? The one with Penny?"

He groaned. "I think you mean Captain Kirk."

"Whatever," she said. "He's the guy in the commercial with the *Big Bang* girl to me."

"Not feeling it?" he asked.

"Actually, it sounds good. I could use some mindless entertainment."

"You know, I just realized there's a lot of horror and thrillers about doctors. *The Island of Doctor Moreau. Dr. Giggles!*" he said as he flipped through recommendations connected to

Visiting Hours.

"Don't give me any ideas," she said. "I'm so hungry and tired right now, I really could go on a murder spree."

He laughed and finally felt his erection subside. This, them being in their groove, was what he was possibly giving up. And for what?

Ryan started the movie and Poppy grabbed a blanket from the end table. She didn't have to say a word—just handed half over to him.

You can do this. It's just Poppy. Why ruin this because of some stupid attraction that's probably fleeting anyway?

By the time the doorbell rang with the pizza, she had moved to the center cushion and dozed off. Her head was in his lap, resting on the pillow. If only she knew the stirring she caused just a few inches below that quilted, flowery throw pillow.

20

POPPY

*P*oppy shrugged out of her jacket, untied her scrub pants and let them fall to the floor. She sat down on the bench in just her underwear and scrub top, too tired to care if any of the other interns came in. She was exhausted, but finally finished with one of the most grueling shifts yet.

Throughout the day, thoughts of her pizza and movie night with Ryan swam through her head. Everything should have been normal. They'd had similar nights ever since she could remember. But something was off, and she couldn't quite place it.

She felt a shift more than anything else. The way Ryan looked at her, and it wasn't just him. Poppy caught herself as she stole glances at him when she thought he wasn't looking. When they caught each other, a shot of excitement and nerves raced through her. Her heart kicked like never before, and try as she might, she couldn't make it stop.

After he'd left and she tossed and turned in bed, she almost reached for her vibrator. It was a gift, perhaps a gag gift, from Sarah years ago. She'd used it a few times. It was a bullet, small and unassuming—and the only thing that brought her to orgasm. She resisted for a moment, knowing she'd just end up thinking about Ryan and that was the last thing she needed.

What the hell, why not? Poppy pulled the vibrator out of the drawer and slid, naked, under the covers. On its lowest setting, she held the vibrator against her nipple and closed her eyes.

One of her hands glided down her belly to her clit, already throbbing. Her wetness had already started to spread. Poppy bit her lip and moved the vibrator to her other nipple.

Suddenly, it was Ryan's hand between her legs. "I love how wet you get," she imagined him saying to her. She spread her legs wider below the covers.

He slapped her clit lightly with his palm and it made her gasp. She put the vibrator on her clit and turned it up a notch. In her mind, it was Ryan who held the vibrator to her, while he kneeled between her legs and stroked himself.

She bucked against the vibrator. Now it was his tongue on her, and he lapped her up like he couldn't get enough. Her insides ached to be filled with him. "You taste so sweet," he whispered up to her. She dove a finger into her pink folds and tasted herself.

Ryan's five o'clock shadow raked lightly across her center, and it made her call out his name. "Tell me you want me to fuck you," he said. She turned the vibrator up another click.

It was all she wanted. "Please," she said. He put just the tip in her opening.

"Is this what you want?" he asked. She turned the vibrator to its highest setting, and he plunged all the way into her.

One hand held the vibrator between her legs, slippery from her wetness, while the other pinched her nipples.

Beside her, the phone buzzed with a text. She glanced at it and saw Ryan's name pop up right as she climaxed. It was hard and intense, enough that it instantly knocked her out.

In the morning, she awoke to a nearly dead phone and a vibrator pressed against her thigh and covered in her dried come.

Her fantasy stuck with her for the entire shift. She was a little shocked about how wildly she'd used the vibrator. It was the first time it had ever made her come like that—maybe the first time she'd really come at all.

Once, when she'd had too much to drink, she'd brought up Will using it on her but he balked at the idea. Embarrassed, even in her alcohol-infused state, she'd never asked again.

Poppy shook her head as she kicked off her ortho shoes in the changing room. Why had she waited so long to make herself feel like that?

"Oh my God, that was a bastard of a shift." Penny slumped down next to her and kicked off her Danskos.

Poppy straightened her back, on high alert. She still felt weird about her last interaction with Penny.

"That Doctor Know-It-All seriously needs to lighten up," Penny said and wiggled out of her scrubs. "As if these shifts aren't beastly enough without her up in our face."

She relaxed. It seemed like Penny wasn't put off by their last conversation after all.

"How's Will doing?" Penny asked as she pulled on jeans. "When's he coming back?"

"Friday or Saturday, just a couple more days," Poppy told her with a smile.

"Yeah? You must be excited. And how are things with Ryan?" Penny didn't look at her, but pulled a threadbare T-shirt over her head. "Is he still trying to mack on you?"

"No!" Poppy said. Even she was aware of how defensive she sounded. "We're just friends—"

"Relax, I'm just playing," Penny said.

Nobody could ever know what had happened between her and Ryan. Especially someone who knew Will. Those lines they'd crossed, the line she'd almost thrown herself across, those had to be their secret for good.

"It's not funny," she told Penny curtly, and pulled on a flowy skirt.

"Sorry," Penny said. Poppy shrugged. "No, for real. I didn't know you were actually mad about it."

"I'm not mad," Poppy said. "It's just annoying. And if people overhear, it might give them the wrong idea."

"I get it," Penny said. "I'll stop. Hey, how about I buy you a drink to make up for it?"

"I'm really tired—"

"We're all really tired." Penny cut her off. "Come on, you can't spend your whole life just working and sitting at home. Have some fun! You only have a few more days before your man's back."

"Seriously Penny, I just wanna go home and—"

"I'm not taking no for an answer," Penny said. "Just one drink. C'mon, it'll be like going to the bar in *Grey's Anatomy.* You can be Meredith."

"Meredith? Seriously? You do know how that storyline ends, right?"

"Fine, do you want to be Christina?"

Poppy sighed. "Alright. I'll be Christina."

"Well, then come on, Doctor Chang," Penny said, and looped her elbow through hers.

"Hey! At least let me put a shirt on," Poppy said.

"Picky, picky. Now we won't get any free drinks." Penny poked at Poppy's breasts spilling out of her satin bra.

They headed across town separately, toward one of the few restaurant pubs that could draw a crowd on a Wednesday night. It was usually a date night spot, but happy hour ran late and they were both on intern salaries.

"There's a spot at the bar," Penny said, and pointed to two stools flanked by what seemed to be college boys on either side.

"You wanna share an appetizer?" Poppy asked her. "Flatbread?"

"Yeah, fine, whatever," Penny replied as she surveyed the room. "This place is dead."

As they sipped on watered-down cocktails and waited for their food, Poppy looked around the bar. It was mostly couples, and the occasional huddle of work crowds. Suddenly, she spotted a familiar pairing across the bar nestled in a booth. Ryan and Sarah were there. Their backs were to her, and Ryan played with Sarah's hair.

Poppy instinctively ducked down a little. As she sized Penny up, she couldn't tell if she'd seen them or not. "What are you doing?" Penny asked.

"Nothing," she said. She forced herself to sit up straight. "Sorry."

Penny gossiped about people at work and complained about their attending physicians. "I mean, she doesn't even try to…"

Poppy completely tuned out and watched Ryan and Sarah from across the bar. Sarah nuzzled his neck and he bit her ear. Surges of jealousy flooded her system. "There's a four-top over there if you want it," the bartender said as he cut into her thoughts. "I can move your tab over there."

"Let's go," Penny said. "These kids are annoying."

"Okay, grandma," one of the boys said to her.

From the table, she had a much better view of the couple. Poppy watched them in profile. They were right in her line of vision as she watched Penny's mouth flap open and shut.

Sarah threw her head back and laughed, which made Poppy cringe. "Are you even listening to me? What are you—"

Penny moved to turn around, and Poppy gripped her thigh. "Don't—"

"Oh. My. God," Penny said, and whipped back to face Poppy with a maniacal grin. "It's them!"

She wasn't certain, but Penny seemed off. Phony. Was this a big performance she'd orchestrated?

"They seem to be getting along really well. Like, really well," Penny said. "What are they doing now? I can't see."

"Nothing," Poppy said. "Talking, laughing." *Why are you reporting to Penny?*

She watched them kiss and saw a flicker of pink between their mouths. They made out in the middle of the restaurant. Ryan's hand moved to Sarah's breast, and she didn't even act surprised. Were they sleeping together? *Don't be stupid, of course they are—they've been seeing each other awhile now.*

"What about now?" Penny probed.

"Shh."

"Tell me! I mean, my God, Sarah is super hot for him. Right?"

"Penny, please."

She couldn't tear her eyes away from them in the booth. And was Sarah… Poppy couldn't believe it. Sarah's hand moved from Ryan's chest, down his stomach and to the bulge of his jeans. It was difficult to see in the darkness below the table, but it looked like Sarah was starting to unzip him. *She's going to give him a handjob right here. Right now. I'm going to watch him get off in Sarah's hand.*

"You have to tell me, I'm dying over here," Penny said. "Can I turn around? Or—"

The excitement in Penny's eyes was unmistakable. She'd known Sarah and Ryan would be here. Poppy didn't know how, but somehow Penny knew. That realization broke the spell cast over her.

"I don't know what game you're playing," Poppy said as she stood up with determination. "But I think it's cruel. Childish, and cruel."

"What are you talking about?" Penny asked with a sniff. "You're acting crazy."

"Apps are here," announced the cheery waitress as she arrived and slid the hot platter onto the table.

"She's paying," Poppy said. Penny's mouth dropped open.

"Seriously, you're going to ditch me here with the bill and a bunch of food that you ordered?" Penny asked. The waitress' eyes widened and she scuttled away.

"Yep," Poppy said. She turned on her heels and made a beeline for the door.

"You're a fucking bitch, you know that, right?" Penny called after her, but she didn't care.

In her car, she struggled to keep the tears at bay. She didn't know if it was seeing Ryan and Sarah or what. Maybe it was Penny. But none of them really owed her anything, so she didn't know why she was so emotional.

Ryan was just moving on like she told him to. Sarah was just being herself. And Penny—well, she was always strange.

"What's wrong with you?" she asked her reflection. Some of the tears had escaped down her cheeks and took what was left of her mascara with them.

Maybe Penny was sort of right. Maybe she was acting crazy. What did it matter to her if Ryan got a handjob in a restaurant? She shouldn't care if Sarah gave him a blowjob or just rode him wild in plain sight.

Maybe she'd imagined the whole Penny thing, too. Sure, she could have known that Ryan and Sarah were at the restaurant. Maybe they'd checked in there or something. But there was no way she could have known they'd be going at it like rabbits.

As Poppy angled toward home, tears stayed on the brim of her eyelids.

When Will gets back, it will be okay. It will all be okay. Everything will go back to normal.

21

RYAN

"So? What do you think?" Li asked Ryan as they finished processing an Aston Martin Vulcan.

"Can't complain," Ryan said. "I was never really into cars, but I have to admit these things are incredible."

"Sweeter than Mia Khalifa's ass, wouldn't you say?" Li winked at him.

"I have no idea who that is."

"You're a better man than me then."

"But honestly Li, thanks for vouching for me. And you know, for hooking it up so I could train with you."

"Not a problem, man," Li said. "I'd take you over some of these jackasses that come through here any day."

Right as Ryan headed to the parking lot, he got a text from Mason. *Want to tube the Shenandoah tomorrow?* Ryan smiled. He couldn't remember the last time he'd hit the river.

Sure, time? he replied.

Early, 8, get a good spot.

Cool.

U got any friends to invite? Ryan knew what Mason wanted, but those days were over. The only women in his life weren't Mason's style.

Still, he shot a text to Sarah, who agreed right away. He knew she would, since she was good like that. Up for anything. *Isn't that what every guy wants? A cool girl who can hang with the guys?*

His thumb hovered over Poppy's number. Why not? He texted her the invite, but knew she wouldn't answer. She'd been acting strange again, even though he thought the movie and pizza night—awkward as it had ended up being—had fixed things. He decided to call her as well, but she didn't pick up either.

"Poppy," he said to her voicemail. "Either call me back, or you'll find me on your steps again." That threat didn't work out as planned. It took him over an hour in rush hour traffic to get back to the neighborhood from his US Marshal post, and by then he was frustrated. Instead of taking his usual turn at the supermercado on the corner, he turned left toward Poppy's place.

By some stroke of incredible luck, her car was parked out front.

"Open up!" Ryan called as he rang the doorbell. He tried to make his voice sound light and joking, but there was a seriousness to it below the surface.

Will opened the door, his mouth set in a hard straight line.

Ryan blinked. "Will. Sorry, man. I thought Poppy—I didn't know you were back."

Will looked at him strangely. "And you're upset that I'm the one who answered the door?"

"No, man, no. You just surprised me is all."

"Okay. So what's up?" Will leaned against the doorframe and held the door with one hand. It was clear Ryan wasn't welcome inside.

"Who is it?" He heard Poppy's voice from the bedroom. She bounded toward the door. "Ryan!" She was stunning, wearing a fitted baby blue dress with a sheer overlay that nipped in at the waist before it blossomed out into a full, knee-length skirt. Poppy looked like a perfectly coiffed housewife from the fifties, but sexier. Hotter. The red lipstick and upswept hair didn't hurt, either.

But it was strange. *Shouldn't they both be tumbled in bed together? Will must have just got back. They haven't fooled around at all?* The idea that all was proper and stoic between them made his heart jump—even though he had no way of knowing what was really going on between them.

"Hey, Pops." Will raised a smug eyebrow at the pet name. "You weren't answering your phone. So…"

Poppy wrinkled her nose. "I've been busy," she said. "As you can see."

"Yeah, I didn't know."

"I'm surprised *Pops* didn't tell you I was coming back this morning," Will said. "I thought you two talked about everything. Being besties and all."

"Will," Poppy said.

"I'm serious! Maybe Ryan could have helped you bake me a welcome home cake or something." The feeble attempt to emasculate Ryan didn't work, but it was more covert than Will's usual approach.

"Good idea. I do love cake, man," Ryan said.

"Will's schedule was bumped around a lot," Poppy said. She directed her words to Ryan, but it sounded like excuses for Will. "I didn't know for sure when he was coming back 'til recently."

"Surprise!" Will said as he raised both brows.

"Yeah. Surprise," Ryan said. "So, how'd it go? Los Angeles, I mean."

"Good, real good," Will said. "A lot of networking, made a lot of connections, so it was a good trip." Ryan could see that California had indeed treated Will kindly. He had a hint of a tan and his hair had lightened a touch.

"Awesome, man. GFY."

"GFY?" Will asked, his head cocked.

Go fuck yourself. "Good for you," Ryan said slowly.

"Ah, good for you. You kids and your textspeak," Will said. He was only a year younger than both Poppy and Ryan.

"Will got some amazing stuff done," Poppy said, desperate to fill the awkward silence. "He met with, who was it? Diablo something—"

"Diablo Cody," Will said, and rolled his eyes at Ryan. "I swear, I don't know how she's a doctor, she can't remember a thing. And I didn't meet with her, Poppy, it was a panel discussion.

A small, private affair and only a few of us were invited, but still."

"Right," Poppy said.

"Diablo Cody, no shit," Ryan said. Poppy shot him a look.

"So. Ryan. What brings you barreling to the door?" Will asked.

"Oh! I just wanted to see… Mason's putting together a tubing thing tomorrow morning. Did you want to come?" He looked at Will. "Both of you, I mean."

"Oh. I don't know—" Poppy began.

"Why not, *Pops*?" Will interjected. "It's one of the first times you've had a weekend off in a long time. Why shouldn't we go?"

She gave Will a curious look. "You want to? I mean, I guess…"

"Great," Will said. "Then it's settled. You know what? Let's invite Penny, too. That way it won't be just a bunch of guys."

"Sarah is coming, too—"

"Even better!" Will said. "I'll message Penny and see if she's free. Maybe we can pick her up?" It sounded like a question, but Ryan and Poppy both knew it wasn't. Will walked away from the door and pulled his phone from his pocket.

A shadow fell over Poppy's face, but she didn't say anything.

"Are you cool with that? With all this… Penny coming and everything…"

"She's fine. Right, Poppy?" Will asked from the couch. "Besides, I already messaged her and she's in."

"Yeah," Poppy said. "Sure. It's fine."

"Come now, Poppy," Will pretended to chide her. "You can't have all the men to yourself."

Poppy blushed.

"Damn, this is a work call. I need to take this," Will said as his phone rang. He went into the bedroom and closed the door.

"Are you really okay?" Ryan said quietly to Poppy. He searched her eyes for a hint of what was wrong. He knew she and Penny had their ups and downs, and it would certainly be strange—to say the least—to see Will tubing. But Poppy had seemed more upset at the idea of Penny coming than Will.

She looked back at the bedroom door. "Of course," she said. When she turned back to him, a smile was stretched across her face. "I'll see you tomorrow."

Before he could respond, she shut the door in his face.

What the hell is wrong with her? With both of them? They were both acting weird—even by Will's standards.

As Ryan slipped into his car, a Snapchat from Sarah came through. *Thoughts?* she asked, and attached an image of her in a skimpy bikini. He had to smile. *This better?* she asked as another photo came through. She pretended her bikini top had fallen off and she covered her bare breasts with a mock look of surprise on her face.

Careful, he replied. *Tubing is serious business. Don't want to give the guys more adrenaline than they'll already have.*

Then this one's just for you, she replied. There wasn't a trace of a swimsuit left in this one.

Ryan laughed as he drove home. Sarah had a way of lightening everything up, but the interaction with Poppy and Will still nagged at him. What was going on with those two?

When he got home, Sarah's Snapchat messages had already disappeared. She pretended like she used the app just because it was fun and trendy, but he suspected she was savvier than she acted. Sarah protected herself, but in a quiet way few noticed.

Hey, he texted her. *Send nudes.* He smiled at their inside joke. When she'd told him "send nudes" was a popular opening line on dating apps, he hadn't believed her. She'd had to show him old messages from her Tinder account.

She replied right away, but on Snapchat.

Text it to me, he said. He could have easily screenshotted it, but had learned quickly after Sarah installed the app on his phone that doing so notified the other person. Besides, it was just creepy.

Naughty boy! she replied. But there was no follow-up photo. They were both silent, a standoff. *Wouldn't you prefer the real thing?* she finally asked. She wasn't very patient. He always won these little games.

Always, he replied.

Want me to come... she asked. She waited a moment before following up with, *over?*

Ryan looked at the clock. It was getting late, and as much as the idea of a warm body sounded tempting, something stopped him.

You'll wear me out for tubing tomorrow, he said. *Need my beauty sleep.*

I'll skip mine if you skip yours.

You don't need it, he said with a winky face, although he hated emoticons. *Pick you up at 7:30 tomorrow.*

Ugh, fine, you're killing me, she said.

In just a few hours, he was going to witness the most bizarre tubing outing that ever existed. He was sure of it.

2 2

———

POPPY

*S*he stood by the river bank and clutched one of the extra tubes Mason had brought. Even this early in the morning, beneath the vanilla sky, the river was swamped with people. All of them, the motley crew she was with included, laughed and splashed as they sailed onto the dark blue waters in their tubes and cheap rafts. A few yards down-river, she watched a gaggle of teenage girls as they launched inflatable unicorns and pizza slices onto the waters.

Murder, she thought. *They should call groups of teenage girls a murder, like crows.*

The morning drive had been tense to say the least. Mason had reserved nearby cabins. It was clear he expected a week-end-long party. Will had complained when the WhatsApp group text decided on busing it from a rural town instead of taking cars up the winding roads. *You'd need a 4WD in some spots,* Mason had messaged.

Still, she had expected Will to complain more than he did. Instead, the lot of them were dropped off at the Shady Pines cabins, walkable to the river's edge.

At the cabins, they shuffled around and dragged their bags full of river gear from room to room. Finally, it was decided—Will and she would share a cabin with Penny and another couple Mason knew from college. With just two bedrooms, one featured a bunkbed and the other a queen-size bed. The couple they bunked up with claimed the private room. Will, Penny and she would share the bunk.

"I should at least get to be on top," Penny said. Neither her nor Will argued.

Poppy changed in the cramped cabin bathroom. As she pulled on her monokini, she listened to Will and Penny as they chatted away. Throughout the morning drive, she'd kept an eye on Ryan and Sarah, too. They seemed like a natural couple as they joked and teased one another. But Poppy had barely said a word to anyone.

"Poppy! Come on!" Will called to her from the river, his tube attached to the floating raft that carried coolers of beer. Slowly she lowered herself, flanked in striped rubber tubing, into the cold water.

She was behind everyone by a few feet. *Why do I feel like the fifth wheel in all this?*

As she brought up the rear, she watched the couples unfold before her. They seemed comfortable alongside the hodge-podge group of bachelors, led by Mason. Will said something to Penny that made her shriek with laughter. Poppy was surprised to find she didn't feel a smidge of jealousy. *Why aren't they together?*

That was a strange thought, but it made sense. They liked each other's company, Penny was quick to dote on Will and feed his ego, and as for Will he seemed to actually like Penny. And Will didn't like anyone. They looked in sync, and made Poppy feel like the intruder. Had it always felt like this?

She floated lazily behind the group. The morning sun started to heat up, warming her skin. Maybe she wasn't the only one stuck at a fork in the road. Down one path might be Will and Penny, and the other was Ryan and Sarah. *But what about me?* She couldn't sit at this impasse forever. She felt stuck, unable to move. The paralysis made her uncomfortable.

The water lulled her into a light sleep, the kind where she was half awake but her body felt too heavy to move. With the sun streamed across her face and the contrast of the cool water on half her body, she let nature have its way with her.

Behind her trailed soft murmurs and giggles. Poppy forced her eyes open and saw that Ryan and Sarah were somehow behind her now. Their fingers were lightly intertwined to keep their tubes together. A bolt of jealousy shot through her. *What do you have to be jealous about?*

"Poppy! Hey," Ryan called. He saw that she had looked back at them. "Come this way."

Sarah smiled at her and released Ryan's hand. Poppy dutifully started paddling toward Ryan as Sarah made her way to Mason's group with the coolers. "Beer?" she called to Poppy, but Poppy shook her head.

"Hi," Ryan said as her tube bumped into his.

She smiled, but didn't say anything.

"Seriously?" he asked.

"What? I'm here."

"Yeah. Here and being a pain in the ass."

"Yeah, well. You don't need me to have a good time. You have Sarah."

"Don't be ridiculous," he said, and tied the strings of his tube to hers.

Why wouldn't he just take her hand like he did Sarah's? She knew how melodramatic she acted, but she couldn't help it. *It's like everyone's ganging up on me these days—even you.*

"Ry!" Sarah called from the floating bar. "Come here a sec." Ryan gave Poppy an annoyed look, untied their rafts and started toward Sarah.

Fine. Let him go. Poppy melted into her pout the rest of the way down the river. By noon, the water started to get fiercer with traces of baby rapids. Poppy knew how to navigate choppy waters thanks to an entire childhood of escaping to the river. However, Sarah started to panic.

"Sarah, stop!" Ryan yelled at her. "You need to stay calm." When Sarah started to get dangerously shaky, Ryan slid out of his tube to steady her. In seconds, his tube was lost down the river and he latched onto Sarah's tube.

"Ryan! You're going to flip us both—"

He let go and was instantly pulled under the water. She couldn't bring herself to move.

En masse, a group of the guys dove into the water after him. Just Penny, Will, Sarah and Poppy remained on their tubes. They locked eyes with one another and continued to float.

Around the bend in the river was a tiny rocky beach. There was no need to speak. The four of them started to paddle like mad toward the shore. By the time they'd all dragged their tubes behind a piece of driftwood on the beach, the guys had followed with Ryan in their arms.

He was limp. Poppy could tell he wasn't breathing.

In the distance, she could hear Sarah's screams, but Poppy was on autopilot. She pushed through the guys and heard someone say, "I'm a doctor, I'm a doctor," over and over. It didn't register that it was her.

"Step back," she said and knelt into the pebbles and rocks. She checked Ryan for any obvious signs of a blocked airway and saw nothing. Like she'd done so many times before, albeit usually with dummies, she tipped his head back and squeezed his nose shut.

Her mouth sealed on his, she forced air into his lungs. "Shouldn't you be pumping his chest?" someone asked. She just shook her head. "I think you're supposed to pump his—"

"His heart's fine," she said, annoyed, as she took her own breath.

It felt like hours, but she knew by her counts it was less than ninety seconds. Ryan started to make choking sounds, and she rolled him onto his side so he could cough the water out of his lungs. *I did it. The kiss of life. I gave him the kiss of life.* She hadn't called it that colloquial term since her pre-med days.

"Hey," Ryan said through ragged breaths. Poppy burst into tears, only somewhat aware that everybody was watching them. He coughed weakly, but wrapped an arm around her in a semi-hug.

"Oh my God! Ryan! Ryan!" Sarah screamed uncontrollably, but Mason held her back. "Are you okay? Are you okay? P, you saved him…"

Everyone else, everything else, faded away for Poppy. When she saw Ryan like that, limp and helpless, all the nonsense she'd mulled over in her head for the past few weeks disappeared.

"Does someone have a phone?" Poppy asked. Tears still streamed down her face.

Wordlessly, one of the guys pulled a phone out of the cooler, wrapped in a waterproof case.

"Do you have service?" she asked. "He doesn't need an ambulance. He's fine. But call us an Uber."

She had no idea where they were, but surely somebody would be on patrol to make some extra scratch off all the kids getting stranded by the riverbank. "It says it's ten minutes away," the guy said. "Anyone else want one?"

Before anybody could say anything, Ryan interrupted. "You all keep on down the river. I'm fine, seriously."

"Ryan—" Sarah started.

"Really, Sarah, I'm fine," he said with a weak smile. "Enjoy yourself, I'm just going to rest it out at the cabin. It's my ego that's hurt more than anything else." He started to act more like himself, which visibly put Sarah at ease.

"Well. If you're sure…"

"I'm sure. I don't think Poppy was having a blast on the river anyway, so she's probably happy for the excuse to duck out early," he said.

She laughed, even through the last of her tears. "You good to walk?" she asked.

Ryan lifted himself up and brushed the pebbles from his back and legs. Poppy linked her arm through his. She couldn't bear to leave his side.

"The driver says mile post twenty-two, just right there," the guy with the phone said, and pointed to the green marker sign up a small hill.

At the marker, Poppy and Ryan watched their group glide back onto the river. "What a day, huh?" Ryan said.

Poppy couldn't wait any longer. As soon as she saw the last of the group fade into the distance, she rose up on her toes and kissed him. He responded like it was natural, expected.

They stood at the roadside, making out like they were sixteen. Ryan squeezed her ass and she pressed into him. His erection was tucked between her thighs, even through his trunks. He rubbed her nipples through her swimsuit and made her whimper.

When he slid his hand down, moving beneath her suit with ease, and started playing with her clit, she wanted it so badly. *This isn't right,* she thought. She couldn't hear any cars coming, but what if someone saw? She couldn't let Ryan get her off in the middle of the street.

Could she?

"What if someone sees?" she whispered to him, but he didn't respond. He just slid her suit to the side and started to flick her clit with his finger. She moaned and opened her legs a little wider.

Ryan slid a finger into her and a Bronco full of teenagers whipped around the corner. She heard them wolf-whistle, followed by a scream to "Get a room!" but they didn't stop.

She made a reach under his shorts, but he stopped her. "Just you," he said. "I want to feel you come on my hand."

As he got her closer, he grabbed the back of her suit and gathered it up tight between her ass. The pressure as it raked across her most sensitive parts brought her closer to coming.

She heard a car approaching from the other side. "Ryan, stop," she said. "I think… that's gotta be the Uber."

Thank God he listened and stepped aside. She barely had time to readjust her suit.

Frustrated, she leaned against his chest as the car pulled over, grateful for the shelter of his body. Nothing else mattered. Not the fact that she was standing roadside in a skimpy suit, what should have been the uncomfortable squish of wetness in her river shoes, or the obnoxious cars that honked and hollered as they drove by.

Ryan's hands rubbed small circles on her back. He didn't let her go until the driver came to a complete stop.

RYAN

"How long?" Ryan asked the driver, a young girl who handled the curves of the road with ease in her little Kia.

"ETA is ten minutes," she said. "You guys get stranded? Tube pop?"

"Something like that," Ryan said.

"There's a towel there if you need to dry off," the driver said. "I always keep a stack when tubing season starts."

She didn't have to tell him twice. He and Poppy both reached for the towel and draped it over their laps. Instantly, his hand was under the towel and between her thighs. "You said ten minutes?" he asked the driver.

"Yeah. You guys want music?"

"Whatever you like," Ryan said. "As long as it's loud."

As the driver cranked up The Chainsmokers, Ryan wrapped a knot of Poppy's swimsuit around his fist—right at her mound. Her eyes got big as he started to slightly jerk the suit up and down. He knew it rubbed every part of her just right, and her eyes started to roll back.

When her breathing got fast, he slowed down and released the suit.

A part of him wanted so much to make her come, right then and there in that stranger's car. Normally the idea would be such a turn-on, but with Poppy it was different. *This is wrong,* he thought to himself. He didn't know if it was this particular moment, or the whole thing. But something was off.

"Your friend already paid," the girl said when she parked outside the cabin. She held up her phone and waved it at them.

"Thanks," Ryan said. He pulled Poppy close to him in the back seat.

He looked up and saw the driver as she stared at him in the rearview. *Did she know what I was doing the whole time?*

"You kids be good," she said as they exited, though she was years younger than them.

This was getting out of control.

The cabin was dark inside. Just a few slivers of daylight poked through. He sat down on the couch and tried not to think about the erection that ached in his trunks. "Poppy, we need to talk—"

But she was already on him. "You can't turn me on like that and leave me hanging," she said as she kissed him. Poppy pulled the upper half of the suit down and exposed her breasts. She played with them as they kissed.

She straddled him. With just thin swimsuit fabric between them, it felt like they were naked. He was fully hard instantly, and by instinct grasped her hips and pulled her firmly against his erection.

Her mouth was on his, and it was just like the first time—like the last time. But now, he knew her body a little better. He could nip and bite at her lips, her neck, and knew exactly how she'd respond.

Poppy let her feet touch the floor, her hands on his thighs, and in one movement she stripped the rest of the bathing suit off her body. Traces of wetness lingered all over her skin. She smelled like the river, like something wild.

He didn't even realize when she leaned over, gripped his trunks and pulled them to the floor. All he could focus on was the complete nakedness of her beautiful body.

It was even better than he'd imagined. Her breasts were like perfect teardrops, accentuated by tight little pink knots of nipples. The shock of the air on her bare skin had made them harden instantly, and he wanted nothing more than to lick and suck on them.

From her breasts to the slight suggestion of a ribcage that topped her incredibly small waist, his eyes roamed farther down. The flare of her hips were perfect for holding onto. And the trimmed small triangle of hair that her bathing suit had barely covered hid what he knew was the sweetest, most addictive treasure he'd ever encounter.

He felt his cock as it began to ache, as it moved from desire and want to sheer need.

Ryan pushed himself to sit on the edge of the couch, grabbed her hips like they were made for him, and brought her center to his mouth. With one arm, he lifted her thigh and placed her foot on the cushion beside him. He had the perfect view of Poppy and her pink, flawless folds.

He flicked his tongue lightly across her clit, coaxed it out of her hood. He heard her moan lightly and felt her fingers as they wove into his hair. That dark blonde hair brushed against his nose. As he worked her clit, his tongue faster and harder, it became impossible to tell where her own juices began and where the remnants of the river ended.

She ground herself into him in rhythmic movements. He was dimly aware of the window right behind him, the window that Poppy faced completely naked. If anyone were to arrive, they'd have a full view of her as she stood, half spread-eagle as she fucked his mouth.

It was like she couldn't get enough of him, and had no inhibitions. She pressed his mouth firmly against her clit, pushed herself up and down, encouraged his tongue to explore her entry. There, the wetness was so intense he had to swallow a mouthful of her to keep his breath. *How can she be this wet?* He opened his eyes, but all he could see was the pink sea of her. "You're amazing," he told her, and looked up. All he could see were her breasts as they shook above his face.

His hands roamed as they wished, sliding up her stomach to cup her breasts. When he went to pinch her nipples, he felt that she already had a hand there. He smiled. She was wild, completely entrenched in pleasure. She played with herself with one hand and controlled the ebb and flow of his head with the other.

Ryan let his thumb take over for his tongue to gaze up at her and take it all in. Her eyes were closed, and she bit her lip. Her hand was on his and she guided his palm from one breast to the other. She sensed his eyes on her, looked down and smiled—the same gapped smile he'd known all his life.

"I want you to come in my mouth," he told her, and went back to licking and sucking her clit.

She groaned louder. He felt her legs, her thighs, as they shook on either side of his head.

When he moved to slide a finger inside her, she shifted away from him. He thought nothing of it. Ryan reached both hands behind her, clutched her round ass cheeks and pulled her closer.

"Ryan," she whispered. "I want you to do it."

In an instant, he pulled her down on top of him. She straddled him like before, but this time there was nothing between them. He gripped his cock, ready to guide himself into her.

"I want you to be my first," she said as she kissed his neck. His tip was pressed against the heat of her clit.

"Your first?" he asked, confused.

"You know…" she said.

"Wait," he froze and she lifted her head to look at him. "You've had sex before, right?"

"No…" she said. "I thought—I mean, I figured you knew that."

Her innocence killed him. *Could that be true? How could that even be possible?* He ran over all their history together, and realized she'd never actually talked about sex. He'd told her all about his first time, but couldn't recall a thing about hers.

"I can't—we can't do this," he said. "We shouldn't do this. It's not right. I can't be your first—especially since you're with someone else… it can't be all sneaky like this. On the sly." He closed his eyes and listened to the words, the excuses, as they spilled out of him. In his head, he knew they sounded right. But in his heart and in every other feral part of him, it sounded weak.

"Ry," she said. She had the power to still everything with just one word. "I want this. I want you." She started kissing him again, and he couldn't resist. Her mouth moved to his jawline and down to his throat. "I need you," she purred into his ear. "I have for so long. Please… "

He knew it wasn't right, not really, but he couldn't stop. *Screw it,* he thought. He grabbed her thighs and in one smooth motion flipped her onto her back. She laughed, and her breasts shook with the motion. On top of her, he made his way down from the hollow of her throat to those idyllic breasts he'd fantasized about for so long.

When he finally took one of her nipples between his lips and rolled his tongue along it, he could feel himself somehow grow even harder. "I fantasized about this," he told her as he kissed his way over to her other nipple.

"Really," she replied with a throaty whisper. She didn't believe him.

"Really," he said. "Not that long ago I jacked off in my shower thinking about this."

She laughed and pressed her groin against him. The heat and wetness between his legs soaked his stomach. He lightly bit and kissed his way back up to her. "I don't want to hurt you," he said as he held himself above her. He rubbed his tip, wet with pre-cum, back and forth along her clit.

"You won't," she said.

He shifted, grasped his shaft and positioned himself at her entry. "Do you want to do it?" he asked.

She smiled, reached down to him, and began to guide him into her.

It was gradual, the kind of excruciating slowness that made him feel everything and need it so much more. She was tighter, warmer and wetter than he could have ever dreamt. He was halfway in and she begged in his ear, "Please." That's all she had to say.

She cried out when he filled her completely, and for a moment he just stayed still, buried deep inside her. He wanted her to set the pace, to dictate what she wanted, what she needed. After a few seconds, she began to search for his lips with hers. Push herself against him. He matched her movements with ease. They moved together in sync as he dove over and over into her.

"You're so tight," he whispered. She felt like perfection.

Poppy's legs were wrapped around him tightly, but she began to loosen. He felt her legs spread open wide to take in all of him. And to give him the best access to her clit. Her hands dug into his back, pulling him in closer, harder and tighter.

"Ride me," he said as he grabbed her waist. He sat her on his lap and as she faced him, her nipples brushed against his face. Poppy held onto the couch cushions and bucked into him wildly. He held onto her hips and sucked on her breasts while he willed himself not to come yet. Not yet. "Are you going to come for me?" he asked her.

She breathed heavily and he could hear the wet slaps between them. She dripped nonstop, like nothing he'd experienced before. She just moaned in reply.

He wanted more than this, more than a tryst on the couch. He needed to fuck her properly.

Ryan cupped her ass and stood up. Her eyes shot open and she intuitively wrapped her legs around his waist. They fucked, slowly, even as he carried her to the bedroom with her arms curled around his neck.

He tossed her on the bed, and she shoved the couple's bags to the floor. As he stood between her legs, opened wide to take him, he couldn't believe how incredible she looked. "You want this?" he teased her.

She gave him a smile he'd never seen before, one of pure hunger.

"I do," she said. He pressed just the tip of himself into her, then peeled open her thighs even wider with his hands.

"Say it, " he told her.

"I want it," she said. He pushed himself an inch into her and she began pulling at her nipples.

"Say you want my cock."

"Ryan!" she said, and a shroud of embarrassment fell over her.

"Come on," he said. He rocked gently, and just barely in and out of her.

"I want your cock," she said quietly. She wouldn't meet his eyes.

"I don't believe you," he said. He was on the edge, about to explode. It was no longer a game. He needed her to say it.

Something in her changed. It happened fast. "I want your cock," she said steadily. Her gaze fastened on his.

It was all he needed. He slammed into her, and Poppy's head dropped back. With one thumb he rubbed her clit as they fucked. Her juices covered his hand, and tiny droplets sprayed across her abdomen. Had she squirted? She was beyond wet, like nothing he'd seen before. Her nails clawed into his thighs. She tried to hold him deeper, and her clit was incredibly swollen. It responded to every touch.

"Are you going to come for me?" he asked her again. She answered with a nod, eyes screwed shut and mouth open.

He lowered himself onto her, could feel her nipples pressed against his chest. She cried out and hugged him closer. Ryan couldn't fathom how he was holding out so long. He was on the precipice, but it didn't matter. He wanted to make this last as long as he could.

His mouth went to her collarbone and he explored every crevice. The sweat between their bodies made her taste saltier than the ocean. He couldn't get enough. "Come for me," he commanded. "Come for me."

"I'm close," she told him. He fucked her deeper, stayed a moment each time at her depths, and she responded.

"Come for me," he told her again.

"Ryan," she said. He felt the quakes tremor through her body. "I'm coming… I'm coming."

He felt her entire world move, and with it he released into her. Ryan cried into her neck, called her name over and over.

He emptied himself into her, and she arched her back when his come shot into her. Her body wanted to drink him all in.

For what must have been minutes, he stayed like that, deep inside her. He felt their combined juices swimming within her. Finally, he pushed himself to the side and panted.

Poppy didn't hesitate. She stood up and walked naked out of the room. She didn't say a single word.

2 4

POPPY

hat the hell was she doing? Poppy had locked herself in the bathroom for the past thirty minutes. She had heard a small shuffling when Ryan finally left the bedroom, but nothing else.

Stupid, she scolded herself. She'd just given her virginity away like that, her "last bargaining chip" as her father would say. *You're a slut.*

Still, there was a bigger part of her that knew it was right. She loved Ryan, there was no denying that—always had. But did he love her like that? As more than a friend? After all, she'd been throwing herself at him like mad for the past few weeks. *Maybe he was just doing you a favor.*

And what about Will? And Sarah? She hadn't given a thought to either of them while she gave herself to Ryan. *What kind of person cheats on her boyfriend and sleeps with one of her closest friend's boyfriend?*

Shouldn't she feel worse than she did? Although Poppy felt worse about Sarah than she did about Will—and that was strange. Her thoughts traveled back to Will on the water, engrossed in conversation with Penny. What was going on with those two? It was no surprise Penny would have a crush on Will, but was it more than that? Was it mutual?

Poppy shook her head. It was probably nothing. What with Penny thinking there was something going on with Poppy and Ryan, it was only natural for her to take Will's side.

Stop it. How can you blame anyone but yourself? She'd learned through counseling in college that having a mother who'd modeled ideal victimization behavior her entire life, had made it pretty easy to slip into that mindset herself.

You're to blame. You. Just you.

"We're back!" she heard Penny's voice crow as the front door flew open. "How are you?"

"Good, I'm better," Ryan said. He must have been sitting on the couch.

"Where's Poppy?" It was the girl half of the couple whose bed they'd just christened.

"Bathroom," Ryan said.

She sighed. It was time to put on the biggest show of her life. She ran the water in the sink and adjusted her hair in the mirror. Poppy tugged at the sarong and tank top she'd grabbed en route from the bedroom to the bathroom. *You can do this. Just act normal.*

"Hey," she said to the group. "How was the rest of the tubing?"

"Great!" Will said. "It was just that one rough patch." His glasses were covered in water spots, and she could already tell he was going to burn, not tan. "You doing alright, Ryan?" he asked. Genuine concern coated his voice.

"Yeah, I'm okay," Ryan said.

"That was some real hero work you did!" the guy half of the couple said. "Going all white knight on Sarah."

Poppy busied herself in the kitchen with Penny. They set up for a family-style meal.

"Whoa!" the girl shouted from her bedroom. "Looks like somebody's been sleeping in our bed." She poked her head out of the room and smiled.

"Oh, yeah, sorry," Ryan said. "I crashed in there when we got back."

"Not a heavy sleeper, huh?" she asked. "I'd hate to share a bed with you."

Poppy could feel Ryan's eyes on her, but she refused to look.

*A*s the entire group settled down on the porch with their plates loaded with burgers, salads and chips, talk turned to the events of the day. "I can't believe you did that!" Sarah said to Ryan.

"Believe it," he said. "I see a girl about to get wet, and I can't help myself."

The guys laughed and the women groaned, but Poppy was sure everyone would catch on. Sarah rolled her eyes as Ryan got his second serving. "The rest of us aren't even halfway done with our first!" she said.

"What can I say? I worked up an appetite this afternoon." His eyes bored holes into her, but Poppy pretended to be engrossed in her food—or, more accurately, her second glass of wine.

"You think you better slow down?" Will asked her.

"Whatever, it's the weekend," she said.

"Now, now," Penny said. She was on Will's other side, and leaned over. She wove her arm through his. "You should listen to your man from time to time."

Will raised his brows at Poppy and nodded in Penny's direction. *See? Why can't you be like that?* his expression seemed to say.

Emboldened with liquid courage, Poppy reached over and slapped Penny's arm away from Will. She tried to do it like she was joking, but even buzzed she was aware it came across as territorial.

"Geez, why don't you just piss on him and mark your territory?" Penny said quietly into her own Solo cup of wine.

"Maybe I will," Poppy said. She leaned into Will and intertwined her own forearm with his.

"A guy could get used to this!" Will said. He beamed at the two women fighting over him. As much as she despised him in that moment, Poppy held onto his arm.

"Hey now, you're all mine," she told him. Poppy leaned over to give Will a kiss and thankfully, he complied. She never knew if he'd play the "PDA is for kids" card or not.

"I should bring you to the woods more often," Will said.

"You want me to get you another beer?" she asked him.

He looked at his nearly empty bottle. "Sure, why not?" As she walked back to the kitchen, he slapped her ass.

"—and, you know, I'm not saying it's a sure thing or anything, but it's promising. Very promising. But you know how contracts in LA are." She'd only been gone a minute, and somehow Will had steered the entire conversation around his work and project. She cringed inwardly, but handed him his beer.

"P? Don't you mind him being gone all the time?" Sarah asked. Her hand rested on Ryan's thigh.

Poppy opened her mouth, but Will cut her off.

"She doesn't mind," Will said. "In fact, she's a great little cheerleader. Maybe my biggest supporter."

"Fascinating," Sarah said. "Does she even talk and walk like a real girl, too?"

Before Will could respond, Penny jumped in. "It's not easy being the girlfriend of a successful artist," she said. "At least, I imagine."

Why am I even with him? He's such a douche. Poppy sat back in the chair and tuned out Will as he continued to blather on about himself. *Is this really the path you're going to choose? Really?*

There was nothing in Will that she wanted for her future. Maybe there never had been, or maybe she'd just been blinded before. Forget choosing Will or Ryan's path, what about her path? Where did that go?

Maybe, Poppy realized, *I've been so far off my own path for so long I won't be able to find my way back. Look at him,* she thought as she took in Will. *He's so full of himself!*

It had been a long time since Will had mentioned it, but he used to be so proud she was going to be a doctor. He'd brought it up every time he introduced her to someone. "This is my girlfriend, Poppy. She's in med school. She's going to be a doctor." At the time, she'd loved it. That was back when she thought being a doctor actually meant something—something more than saving people. As if that weren't incredible in itself.

She shook her head. She was so offtrack. *Will only wants you because having a doctor on his arm makes him look good.*

But she wasn't in this fantasy alone. She'd looked a little too long at advertisements for engagement rings. She'd dropped hints she liked the halo style, and had told Will she thought yellow gold was charming and coming back in style.

Stop lying to yourself. Okay. All of that was true, she had to admit. But the biggest truth she'd buried from herself? She'd ached for the day Will and her would have a baby—not to start a family, but to quit her life. Will would make it big, they might even move to Hollywood, and she'd spend her days at Mommy and Me classes while she swapped advice with other Sweaty Betty-bedecked moms.

You're a fraud. Uncomfortable, and with a head swarmed with wine, she stood up. "Guys, I think I'm gonna rest for a bit," she said.

"You okay?" Sarah asked, concerned. She rubbed Ryan's knee.

"Yeah," Poppy said as she avoided Ryan's gaze. "I'm just tired."

She was barely curled up onto the bottom bunk when Will appeared in the doorway. "What's the matter with you?" he asked. "You just up and left me out there."

"I'm tired, Will," she said.

"I don't know what's wrong with you," he said. With a heavy sigh, he sat on the bed next to her. "I was going to wait to tell you this when we weren't in the middle of nowhere, when you were in a better mood, but it looks like you're never going to be in a good mood anymore."

"Tell me what?" she asked. *You're leaving me for Penny.*

"The script was picked up," he said. "I'm moving to LA."

"You're—you're leaving?" she asked, and sat bolt upright in bed. "So, we're… "

"Don't be silly!" he said. "There's no reason for us to split, not if you don't want that. You're coming with me. There are hospitals in LA, aren't there?"

"Well, yeah," she said. "But it's not—I'm an intern, Will. I don't get a say in where I am. Do you remember how hard it was to even get this internship? And even if I was a full-fledged doctor, it's not easy to—"

"You just can't be happy for me, can you?" he asked. "It's always all about you."

"Will! How can you say that? I—"

"Just admit it," he said. "This has nothing to do with your internship or anything else. I'm sure you could find a way to finish your internship in LA… if you wanted to. I mean, assuming you're not wanting to stay here because of Ryan—"

"Oh geez Will, no. Okay? It has nothing to do with him."

"Good! Then it's settled. And there's no reason for you not to say yes."

"What?"

Will stood up and dug through his suitcase. He pulled out a black velvet ring box and tossed it toward her. Inside was a pear cut diamond in a platinum setting. Poppy looked up at him, unsure. He didn't move, a challenge to her loyalty.

Unable to speak, she slipped the ring on. It was too big, and felt like dead weight.

"Just think about it," he said as he moved to her and patted her head. "Our future could be great. You'll see."

Like a hawk, he swooped down and kissed her hard on the mouth. It was tight-lipped and rigid. He smiled, turned around, and walked back to the patio. Poppy stayed, alone, in the dark.

25

RYAN

*R*yan knocked on her door, and didn't give a damn if Will was there. It had been two days since the tubing trip, and she'd pulled that crap of pretending to be the doting little girlfriend the entire time. And that proposal—if you could call it that? Poppy coming out of the bedroom with that ring wrapped around her finger and looking miserable? Ridiculous. Yet there was still something about it that unnerved him.

"What?" she said, sleepy-eyed when she opened the door. "Ryan, it's like midnight—"

"I know what time it is." Her eyes opened wide, and he knew Will wasn't there. She was in nothing but a thin T-shirt that didn't even cover the triangle of her panties. And there wasn't a ring in sight.

"Ryan—"

He shut her up with a kiss. His mouth consumed hers while his hands roamed to her breasts. Ryan pulled at her nipples through the shirt and she whimpered. They were in the doorway, but he didn't care who saw. His hand traveled down, across her stomach and over the silkiness of her panties. They had already started to soak through. "Wet already?" he said with a smile. She bit her lip and pushed harder against him.

Poppy tried to pull him inside, but he held her steady. In an instant, he was behind her, her wrists pinned easily in one of his hands. With his free hand, he ran his fingers up her shirt and exposed her abdomen to the city below. There was nobody on the streets, no neighbors looked through windows—at least that he could see. Poppy stiffened in his arms, but her passion surpassed any shyness or embarrassment. He kissed her neck and she let her head go heavy, leaned it back and rested it on his chest.

When his hands moved from her unbelievably hard nipples down toward her underwear, she gave a feeble attempt to free her hands. "Be good," he whispered to her, and she complied.

He could tell just by touch that those yellow panties were stained dark by her wetness. Ryan drove his throbbing cock into her ass through his jeans while he flicked a finger across her clit—even with the silk material in the way, she started to shake.

"You like that?" he asked her, and she whispered a yes as he pinched her folds together. He slid his hand underneath her underwear, across the slickness of her clit, and his finger dove into her warm, wet folds.

He fucked her with his hand, one finger and then two, while his thumb circled her clit. "Spread your legs," he told her and she did without hesitation. She stepped wider in the doorframe, faced the street below without question, and let him have his way with her easier. The entry light lit them both up, but especially her. "I want the world to see you belong to me," he said as he drove his cock into her backside.

He released her hands and moved his own to her ass, squeezed her cheeks and spanked her lightly. He dove into her panties from behind, and easily slid his fingers into her. She started to moan and bend forward, but he caught her waist with his other arm and held her upright. Unable to move, she started to rub her clit with one hand—and reached behind to unzip his jeans with the other. "Is that what you want?" he whispered in her ear.

"Yeah," she said. She fumbled to unzip him with one hand. He fucked her faster with his hand.

"Tell me, " he said. "Tell me what you want."

"I want your cock," she said quietly.

"Say it louder."

"I want your cock," she said. It was a normal level and even as she continued to rub herself and cover his hand in her wetness, he felt her look around.

"Louder," he said. She was quiet, and his hand went still but his arm was still clenched around her waist. Poppy started to wiggle against his hand. He grabbed her hand that worked her clit and forced her into stillness. "Louder," he repeated.

"I want your cock!" she shouted into the night. He freed her hand, drove his fingers into her two more times, and pulled her into the apartment.

They didn't even make it into her bedroom—he didn't think either of them could wait that long. Instead, he lifted her onto the kitchen counter and fell to his knees. Easily, he tore the underwear off of her, and she spread her legs eagerly.

He kissed her inner thighs and she squirmed. Ryan loved her frustration when he teased her. Gingerly, he kissed her clit and she pushed, demanding, against him. "Come on," she said.

"Come on, what?"

"Ryan—"

"I know you want my cock. And you'll get it, I promise," he said. "But what about right now? What else do you want?"

She whimpered and reached for his head.

"You want me to eat your pussy?" he asked.

"Yeah."

"Then you know what to say," he said, and took her between his lips.

"I want you to eat my pussy," she said, and opened her legs even wider.

Ryan drove his tongue between her legs and breathed in her scent. She tasted like a sweet addiction he'd never known he needed. As her thighs rested on his shoulder, her hands on his head, she pulled him back to her every time he pulled away.

Her hands held his face so close to her he could hardly breathe, but he didn't care.

"I'm close," she said. "I'm close. Ryan—"

"Come in my mouth," he said. He barely got the words out before she covered him in her juices, as small streams of her sweetness shot into his mouth and covered his face. It almost made him come right then and there, but he held himself back.

"Oh!" she said. He looked up from between her thighs and saw she was embarrassed. "I didn't…"

She didn't know she did that. She was a virgin, that was surprising enough. But to think she'd never gotten herself off properly was shocking. "Taste yourself," he said, and stood up. He cupped her chin in his wet hand and slipped his tongue into her mouth. "See how sweet you are?" he whispered.

She relaxed and kissed him back. He ran a finger across her swollen folds and she shivered. "Too sensitive?" he asked.

She shook her head. "I'm good," she said. "Just give me a minute. Let me take care of you—"

Poppy began to finish her job of unzipping him, but he stopped her. "Tonight, it's all about you," he said. He unzipped and stepped out of his jeans. She reached for his cock like it belonged to her, and it felt natural. Ryan pulled his own shirt over his head and then removed hers.

"I want to," she said, and looked down at him almost shyly.

"Have you ever…"

He knew it was a stupid question, but he had to ask. She shook her head. "Tell me how," she said.

She hopped off the counter and kissed her way down his stomach and licked his tip. Just feeling her mouth on him, even this small amount, was electrifying. She played with taking him in deeper. "Wrap your lips around your teeth," he told her, and she did. "Good," he said.

He watched her, on her knees below him, unable to believe it.

"Hold the base," he said, "like this." He grasped the base of his shaft and she placed her hand over his. "Tighter," he said.

Slowly, she worked up to take him farther into her mouth. Every time she came up, she made a thirsty sound like she couldn't get enough. The next time she took him in her mouth, she released her hand and he felt himself hit the back of her throat. "Fuck, Poppy," he said.

She licked him up and down, eventually moving to his balls which tightened at her touch. Poppy looked at him with a question in her eyes, and he nodded. She stroked him with her hand while she kissed and sucked his balls.

"I'm almost there," he said.

"Good."

"No. Not like this. I want to come inside you."

She smiled and crawled back up to him.

They kissed like teenagers as he lifted her back on the counter, for what felt like hours. Every now and then, his tip brushed against her heat, but he pulled back when she shivered. Still too sensitive. "We don't have to do this," he said.

"I want to," she said. "Just wait for me… "

He nipped at her neck and sucked a hickey below her ear.

Finally, he tested her opening and found that she pressed against him. "Seems someone is ready for round two," he said.

She nodded, and he took a step back. "I want you to watch," he said as he pressed her thighs open wider. They both looked down and watched as he slowly slid his length into her. Poppy started to close her eyes when he was halfway in, and he stopped. "Watch," he told her. "Watch how hard you make me. How wet you are. How we fit like this." She opened her eyes and watched herself take him all the way in.

Ryan pressed hard against her, and she called out. "That's your G-spot," he told her, and he felt her nails dig into his shoulders.

He held onto her hips and thrust into her slowly, in tempo with her moans. When her breath quickened, he began to fuck her faster.

"Ryan," she called, over and over again. Every time she said his name, it brought him closer to orgasm.

She was so wet, he lost track of where she began and he started, but it didn't matter. The sound of their skin as they slapped together was all he could hear. That, and Poppy's moans and his name as it rolled out of her mouth.

As he started to get close, a blast of rationality shot through him. "Oh, shit," he said, but he couldn't stop fucking her. She felt too good. "Are you on something? Do you take—"

"Come in me," she said. Those three words were all he needed to hear. He cried out when he filled her up, and the shot of him inside her brought her to orgasm all over again. He could feel the wave of her coming, the throbbing of her walls. It squeezed his shaft, forced every last bit of his come into her.

"Jesus," he said, and she held him closer.

"You feel so good," she said. "It feels so good." He held onto her, and slid in and out of her, half-hard. With every pulse, he made her shake all over again. He could do this forever.

She kissed him as she rolled through the last waves, and he felt their juices start to run down his leg.

"I want to taste it," she said.

"What?" he asked, confused.

"Let me clean you up," she said. He was too worn out to argue. Poppy slipped off the counter and onto her knees. She licked him softly and tasted the blend of them together.

"Gentle," he said. She didn't stop until she'd finished every last drop.

"So," he said as they moved to the couch, without a thought to getting dressed. "Is he…"

He wasn't sure how to bring up Will, but he had to ask.

"He's gone," she said.

"Gone?"

"Back to LA."

"Oh."

"You staying?"

"What?"

"Are you staying?" she asked again, slower this time.

"If you—if you want me to."

She just smiled. "Of course I want you to," she said. "Come on." She stood up, took his hand and led him into the bedroom.

Curled up in her bed, he couldn't believe his luck. She was perfect, always had been. *Why the hell did it take you this long to see it?*

His hand grazed over her breasts as they lay side by side. Her nipples hardened at his touch, but he couldn't get over the hickeys that covered her chest. They were his marks, his proof she was his. "You look like you got your butt kicked," he said.

She giggled. "Yeah. I think it'll be awhile before I can wear a swimsuit again."

"I think it looks good," he said.

"Yeah? Maybe I should return the favor then." She started to kiss and bite his neck. He wanted her to mark him, for everyone to see. He'd take her as long as he could have her.

26

POPPY

When she woke up, the first threads of dawn had woven into the night sky. Poppy fluttered her eyes open. She could feel the heat their two naked bodies made. Ryan was spooned behind her, his arm wrapped protectively around her waist. She sighed, and felt him start to harden between her thighs. They didn't have to say anything.

As if it were choreographed, she started to push her ass into him. He tightened his grasp on her waist—he was inside her in seconds.

Poppy moaned as his shaft stroked her G-spot and moved a hand to circle her clit. Ryan bit her shoulder lightly. Her legs blossomed open automatically, and he tucked one knee beneath hers to open her wider.

She took in the last of the night sky as he fucked her, slow and steady from behind. On the nightstand, inches from her face, were two photos. One was of her and Will at a friend's birthday party. Will's smile was forced, as always. The other was of her and Ryan at high school graduation. It was one of her favorites, with his arm wrapped around her as they laughed wildly.

Guilt started to seep into her just as Ryan pushed himself up and grabbed both of her thighs to flip her face down. He directed her to pull her hips into the air. Balanced on just her forearms and knees, she pushed the photos out of her mind as he started to kiss and nibble at her cheeks.

"I want to taste every part of you," he said.

When his mouth roamed to her ass and she felt his tongue start to rim her, she gasped and closed her eyes. She knew the last of the moonlight that shone through the window lit up her fair skin, that Ryan was getting an unprecedented view of her most intimate parts, but she didn't care. She wanted him to have it all, to see it all.

He had one finger on her clit, moving it back and forth while he kissed and licked a piece of her she'd never considered. It excited her in an incredible way, an unexpected one. But she needed more. She wanted him inside her again.

Poppy raised her hips higher and encouraged his mouth toward her opening. Ryan laughed behind her. "You're insatiable," he said, and obliged. When he plunged his tongue into her wet center, she cried out. Poppy put her hand over his, made him work her clit faster.

When she was on the edge of coming on his tongue, Ryan moved to his knees and slapped his cock against her ass. Somehow, he knew he shouldn't tease her for long this time and slid into her wetness. He called out her name when he hit her depths and she bit down on the edge of the pillow.

Ryan held tight to her hips, but soon fell over her. She could see her breasts hung heavy below her, and watched as Ryan reached below with one hand to cradle them as they bounced.

As her orgasm built inside her, she turned her head and looked at the photo once more. Miraculously, she managed to block out the one of Will and focused solely on her and Ryan. He looked the same to her now as he did then. She couldn't believe he was inside her at this moment, about to shoot himself into her.

"You want me to come inside you?" he whispered into her ear. Like he could read her thoughts.

"Yes," she said. *More than anything.*

"What'll you do for it?" he asked, a smile in his voice. He slowed his thrusts, and slowed her impending orgasm in the process.

"Anything," she said as she tried to bounce herself into him at a faster clip. But he was too strong, too big for her to control from this angle.

"Anything?" he asked, and gathered her hair in his fist. He was on his knees again. Lifted by her hair, he made her rise up to her hands. She was on all fours and he governed her like she was an animal.

Him being in total control of her like that, body and mind, excited her beyond belief. "Anything you want," she repeated. Warm trickles of her arousal started to inch down her inner thighs.

"I can't believe how wet you are," Ryan said. He slid in and out of her slowly, her hair held tightly in his hand. She could tell that he watched himself as he disappeared in her, over and over.

"Anything," she said again, quieter this time. Her eyes were closed, her neck arched and exposed.

"Tell me you're mine," he said. He started to fuck her faster and made her breath speed up.

"I'm yours," she said. There was no hesitation.

"This is mine," he said. He let go of her hip briefly to spank her ass, hard and sharp. The bite of pain shot her to the edge of orgasm. For just a moment, she was held up solely by his hardness deep inside her and his hands in her hair.

"It's yours," she said.

She felt his heat burst into her and he let go of her hair. Before her forearms hit the bed, she was already coming, her insides clenched onto him tight.

Ryan fell onto his back beside her as she lowered to her stomach. When she looked at him, her eyes went to the photo frames. Both of them. "Want to get cleaned up?" she asked.

He smiled and ran a hand across his half-hard cock. "I think I need to give it a rest," he said.

"I didn't mean that," she said as she swatted his arm. "Shower. We could probably both use it." Really, she just needed to get away from that photo.

Ryan got up first, and she covertly shoved the photo behind a stack of books.

He opened the window in the bathroom and let the dawning light illuminate them. She could tell neither of them were ready for the harsh brightness of the real world. *Please, extend the magic just a little bit longer.*

As he trailed the soap across her body, he lingered at her breasts. But Poppy's mind was elsewhere. She couldn't stop thinking about the ring crammed in the nightstand drawer. It screamed at her to do something with it. "Hey," Ryan said over the hiss of the shower. "Where are you?"

She blinked her eyes open. "Right here," she said, and forced a smile.

He looked beautiful in that morning light. *Magic hour,* she'd heard directors call it. Nearly every movie had at least one scene filmed at either dawn or dusk. It was when magic was promised. Yet the majority were at dusk because the night felt so wild and mysterious. Dawn was beautiful, but like the calm before the storm.

She bit her lip and drank him in with her eyes. The rolling muscles of his shoulders and the light spray of hair across his chest. Part of him was so clearly a man. She couldn't recall when he'd packed all those muscles on, or when his abs had become as hard and cut as steel. Yet she could still see the high school jock in him, the sweet softness he used to cover in raglan shirts and letterman jackets.

"See something you like?" he asked with a laugh. She blushed, caught looking at his chest and stomach.

"Pops," he began. She sucked in her breath. *Don't start this conversation. Please don't start this conversation.* "We need to talk about everything…"

Suddenly she felt incredibly vulnerable. Violated. Poppy was acutely aware not just of her nakedness, but of how swollen she still was between her legs. Their cocktail of juices still ran out of her. Standing here with Ryan in a cramped stall was not where she wanted this to happen.

Maybe you don't want this to happen at all. Anger poured through her. *Why are you ruining this?*

"Just be thankful for now," she said with a snap. His eyes widened and she slid open the shower door with a slam. She didn't even check to see if anything broke, but padded out of the bathroom without a towel. She felt the slap of her wet footsteps against the wood floors as the water in the bathroom turned off.

She slammed the bedroom door, cursed herself for never getting the lock on it fixed, and shut herself in the poor excuse for a walk-in closet. As she flipped on the glaring lights, the last of the night's enchantment faded away.

The door to the bedroom clicked open. "Poppy?" Ryan called, confused.

"Just a minute," she replied, and willed her voice to sound normal.

"I'm going to go get some coffee and bagels from down the block. Be right back."

When she was sure he'd left, she crept out of her closet and sat down by the nightstand. Carefully, she pulled the photo of her and Will out from behind the books and put it back in its place. Poppy took the ring out of the drawer. It was hidden behind her vibrator and a handful of condoms she'd taken from the student health center years ago. They must have expired ages ago.

You really are an ugly ring, she thought to herself, and instantly felt even guiltier. *Who cares about the ring? It's the intention that matters.*

That was the other thing. What was Will's intention behind this? Had she been too subtle in the hints about her tastes? Was this all just stupidly materialistic on her end? It felt like he'd intentionally chosen a ring he knew she'd hate.

What in the world are you doing?

RYAN

Ryan took another swallow of coffee as he sat on his tiny balcony. With just the little steel table and chair squeezed onto the space, it was a small slice of a retreat, but it was his. Papers from the US Marshals were fanned out before him, held down by his phone.

There were a number of urgent vacancies available around the country. All immediate openings were for overseeing WitSec persons or hunting fugitives. *Clearly, there's a reason so many of these posts are going unclaimed.* He thought back to what Lieutenant Stevens had said about the Marshals program being starved for new recruits.

He enjoyed the work with Li, but it wasn't particularly challenging. That adoration of exotic cars just didn't have the same pull in him it seemed to with other men. Plus, it was very much considered a training post with no promise of long-term or full-time employment. He was technically a contractor with zero stability. Ryan pushed another paper with an opening description under the pile he'd already pored over.

If he left the car post, would Poppy even care? Maybe it would be easier for both of them, and she could slide right back into that pre-packaged life with Will.

Ryan shook his head. *Melodramatic much?*

Still, he felt like shit after the way they'd parted the other day. He'd returned from the corner shop with Americanos plus bagels and lox, Poppy's favorite, and they'd eaten in silence. When he'd made an excuse to leave, she'd barely looked at him.

Since when did they connect best in the bedroom? It was exactly what he'd been afraid of—their friendship falling apart. And for what? Some good times between the sheets.

No. Some fucking incredible times between the sheets.

His phone lit up with Sarah's name. Funny, he didn't even feel a stir of excitement. Granted, he'd been breadcrumbing her at best since the tubing trip. *It's not her fault. She doesn't deserve that.* He knew he should break it off with her, but he couldn't. He'd never been good at walking away from relationships, even casual ones, but this one was particularly thorny.

The lies have to stop, he thought. *The lies to yourself, and the lies to everyone else.*

It was obvious he wanted Poppy. Obvious to him, to Will, and hell, it had to be obvious to Poppy, right? She was all he could think about.

The phone began to ring, and it made his heart race. He wasn't ready to have the talk with Sarah, not yet. His nerves settled when he saw it was the strange "1111" number that could only be Eli.

"Yes, Mr. President," he answered.

Eli laughed on the other end. He always sounded funny calling from the office. "Just making sure you're okay," he said. "After you nearly drowned in, what was it, six feet of water, Navy SEAL?"

"Those rapids are a trip when you're a six-pack deep," Ryan said. "Why are you calling me from the Big House, anyway?"

"You mean the White House," Eli said. "I'm sure there's a whole orchestra listening in, so let's keep phrases like 'Big House' to a minimum, huh?"

"Right, right," Ryan said. "So, what's up?"

"You mean besides the whole world keeping an eye on me like a grumpy schoolteacher? Not much. I could use some discourse on the real world, though. Tell me how civilian life is treating you."

Ryan considered a safe play, but the events of the past few weeks overwhelmed him. If he couldn't talk to his brother about this crap, who could he vent to? "More drama over here than Afghanistan," he said.

"Oh yeah? I said no disturbances," Eli said coolly.

"Excuse me?"

"Sorry, talking to one of the interns. But really, what's up?"

"It's… I don't know, man. My 'love life' if you want to put a term to it."

"Oh, I see," Eli said. "You falling in love, finally? Who is it? That Sophia girl who's always tagging you?"

"Who? Oh, you mean Sarah—no, not her."

"Really? I mean, I'm not Facebook stalking you or anything, but you two have looked pretty chummy these past few weeks. She's cute," Eli added.

"Yeah. She's a great girl."

"So it seems the SEALs couldn't slow down your playboy roll after all then. What's the flavor of the month's name?"

"Poppy."

"Poppy? Like, the Poppy? The one who's been your best friend forever?" Eli was clearly shocked. That couldn't be a good sign. If the President of the United States thought this was dramatic, what would everyone else think?

"Yeah, how many people named Poppy do you know?" He was on the defensive, but couldn't help it.

"Okay, chill out. How do you… what… does she… doesn't she have a boyfriend?" *Is that the best you can do?*

"Technically, kind of a fiancé now," Ryan said.

"Jesus, Ryan. You need to walk away from that."

"I can't," he admitted. "I think I'm in too deep now."

"How far has it gone?"

"Um, well, 'all the way' I guess you could say."

"You're sleeping together?"

That's an understatement. "Yeah," he said.

"And that Sophia girl? You at least broke it off with her, right?"

"Not exactly…"

"Shit, Ryan, you've made a mess."

"It gets worse."

"How does it get worse?"

"Well, I know you never knew Poppy that well or anything. And I didn't know this either until really recently. But—"

Ryan didn't know if he should tell Eli or not. But it wasn't like Eli would go blabbing around town, and already there was a weight lifted off of Ryan's shoulders just by sharing this much. "But what?" Eli prodded.

"She was a virgin?" It was out now.

"What do you mean she was a virgin? Wait, isn't she your age?" The confusion in Eli's voice was thick.

"I mean the other night…"

"Ryan, stop." Stop. He wished he could.

"I'm in deep," Ryan admitted. "I don't know what to do."

"And it's not just the sex?" Eli asked.

"No," Ryan said, nearly offended.

"Calm down, I was just asking. Because, you know, the whole taking someone's virginity thing can be a trip for some guys—"

"Eli, come on. You know me better than that."

"You're right. Sorry. But what about your friendship? I mean, you two have been glued at the hip since you were kids."

"I know," Ryan said. "I know. I'm—I'm not even sure there will be anything left after all of this. But I need to find out. I'm willing to risk it." It was true, though the first time he'd realized it.

"And Poppy?"

"I need to find out if she's willing to risk it, too. Once and for all. This has gone on long enough."

"You're telling me," Eli said. "I have to tell you, I always wondered. In high school and everything. You seemed almost too close, you know? I figured you were boning like mad and just keeping it a secret for whatever reason."

"Boning, Eli? Really? Is that how the POTUS talks?"

"It is when he's talking to his brother and wants to give the phone observers something to gossip about."

"I just, I don't want to hurt anyone. You know? Especially her. And Sarah. They—neither of them deserve any of this."

"If you really want this," Eli said, "if you're sure, go for a grand gesture. Women love that sort of thing."

"You mean like a proposal?"

"No, you idiot! Besides, isn't she already engaged?"

"Oh. Yeah," Ryan said.

"I mean—sorry, I don't mean to make light of it. I just mean, not anything like that unless you're really, really ready for it. I know you've been tight with her for years, but there's no reason to jump straight from friends to marriage."

"Yeah, you're probably right."

"If this all works out, if you end up together, enjoy it. You know? Date! Have fun. Make up for some of those lost years."

Lost years. Ryan had never thought of it like that. Had they really wasted so many years? In a way, maybe Eli was right.

But on the other hand, no time spent with Poppy, whether it was just friendship or not, felt wasted.

"Yeah. But a grand gesture like what?" He'd never felt the need to do something like that before. Then again, all of his former relationships had been easy and casual. The women had never acted like they expected anything more. Of course, maybe that was normal. What else would a girl expect if she dated someone who was constantly on tour?

"Something real," Eli said. "A genuine step forward, together. Just talk to her, Ryan. Make a declaration."

"A declaration, huh? There's some polititalk for you."

"You know what I mean," Eli said.

"Yeah, I do."

"I said no dist—oh. Alright." Eli's voice was muffled as he barked at whoever was in the office. "Hey, Ryan, I have to go. But keep me posted, okay? And I don't want to see any more smoochy pictures of you and that Sophia girl online, okay?"

"Yeah, yeah. Go govern the free world," Ryan said.

"Talk later." Eli was gone.

He kicked his feet onto the balcony railing and started mulling over ideas. Scenes from cheesy movies flew through his head. Skywriting from a plane, hot air balloon rides with champagne, a penthouse suite at the fanciest hotel in D.C. filled with flowers.

That's way over the top, he thought. Worse, it wasn't Poppy. It wasn't him. It wasn't them.

He sat up and knocked over the last of his coffee onto the papers. He knew what to do.

2 8

POPPY

*P*oppy sucked in her breath and filled her lungs as she pulled up to her parents' house. It was the last place she thought she'd go, but it was funny how when your world falls apart you seek out childhood comforts.

"Of course you can come home!" her mother had said over the phone.

"And Dad?" Poppy had asked.

"He doesn't get home from the ba—he won't be back until night," her mom said. She caught herself, but it was no secret her dad spent all day at the local dive.

Poppy climbed the steps and tried to ignore the cobwebs. Even though she'd just been there recently, the house still seemed smaller and shabbier. The incredible shrinking house.

She didn't knock, just walked right in. That was a first in nearly fifteen years. It felt like home again—but only for an instant.

In the living room, her mother was perched anxiously on the edge of the couch. She held what seemed to be a scarf in mid-crochet in her hands. The hook looked deadly. On the recliner was her dad.

Her mom offered a tight-lipped smile, but her father just glared at her. On the television, canned sitcom laughter broke out.

"What are you—what are you doing…"

She couldn't choke the words out.

"Will called, honey," her mom said.

"Will? Why? When did he—"

"To ask for your goddamned hand," her father said gruffly.

"The start of last week…" her mom trailed off.

"Came down here. In person," her dad said. Anger boiled right below the surface. "Called first. Like a gentleman should."

"He was very nice," her mother said softly. She looked, yearned, at her daughter. Poppy could see a bruise, faded to violet, that hugged her mother's eye. She'd done a shoddy job with the concealer.

"Shut up," her father snapped to her mother without looking at her. Poppy scanned her mother's body, or what she could see of it, and saw what looked like strangulation marks that peeked out from the turtleneck.

Her mom's mouth slammed shut.

"Your mother is right about that, though," her dad said. "He was nice. Brought flowers and candy for her. Bourbon and cigars for me. From Cuba."

Poppy nodded and took in the rules of the game. She couldn't remember if she'd shut the front door completely, or if it could easily be pushed open if she had to run. *Why did you wear heels? What were you thinking?*

"That boy of yours promised us, *promised* us, you'd be taken care of. He's got some crazy idea, for some strange reason, you deserve that. A kept woman." Her dad shook his head, and his wiry gray eyebrows quivered with him. "Even offered your old man a job with a 'real up-and-comer in the TV industry.' That's what he said. And you know what?"

He looked at her like he expected an answer. "What?"

"I believe him. I don't know why, but he wants to take care of you. Of all of us." So that was it. Will had cornered her in the way she least expected. He got the monster of her childhood in on it, and they came at her from both sides.

"Dad," she started. "I—"

"You what?" he asked and stood up. She was taller than him now. *When did that happen?* However, those childhood scars ran deep. He tore terror through her with just his tone.

"I love that boy, you know that?" her father asked. The surprise on her mother's face was almost comical. "Love him like my own flesh and blood."

Poppy searched for words, but none came. She'd never heard her dad say that word before. Not to her mother, and certainly not to her.

"You do?" she asked her mom, incredulous. She'd always acted indifferent about Will.

"Well, I wouldn't say that—"

Poppy was surprised at how much she could read into those five short words. For once, her mom's voice was smooth and strong. *She didn't like Will.*

"Don't act like a bitch," her father said sharply. "Always rurnin' everyone's good time. Jealous is all," he said to Poppy. She hated how he said that. *Rurnin'.*

"I just meant—"

"One more word," her father warned her mom. *Is that what happened? Did Mom try to help me, tell Dad she didn't like Will? And he let her have it, because of me?*

"Any time attention's off her – well, you know how your mom is." She couldn't believe what he said.

Poppy couldn't find the right words. Her mom? Jealous? Petty? Her dad was really reaching.

"And the job? It would be a real boon, I know it," he continued.

"Dad, I—"

Stop stammering like a little girl. "And your mother'd be a whole lot happier. A lot *safer.* With me working."

There was the rabbit punch. "I… I…"

"But only if y'all get married, of course," her dad said. "You are getting married. Aren't ya." It wasn't a question.

"I don't… you know, it's all really fast?" She could hear her voice lilt up, like a child's. "Both of our careers are just starting. You know? Maybe, I mean… I think it might be better if we took some time? Just—"

"Don't you bullshit me. You're gonna marry that boy. If you got any goddamned sense in you."

"I don't… "

"Where's that ring?" her father asked suddenly. She glanced down at her bare hands. Thank God she'd slipped the box into her pocket. "Put it on. Show your mom," he demanded.

She slid the ring onto her hand. It felt cold and foreign. Poppy held out her hand limply.

"Closer," her father demanded. "Can't nobody see it from here."

She took a step toward him.

"Your mom, you goddamned idiot," he said.

Poppy changed directions, but kept watch on her father from the corner of her eye.

"Now, ain't that something," her father said. Poppy and her mom both nodded.

"I said ain't that something," he repeated.

"Yes." Their voices blended together. Fear made a beautiful medley.

"You keep that on, like you're supposed to."

"It's loose," Poppy said.

"What?"

"It needs to be resized."

"Bullshit. It's fine. 'Cause you don't eat enough is all." Her father slouched back down into his chair.

"Do you want some supper?" her mom asked. Her voice was soft but her knuckles were white as they clenched the crochet hook.

"Um—"

"Well, would you look what time it is!" her father said as *Shameless* came on. "Bourbon time. It's five o'clock here."

Everyone acted like he hadn't been drinking the whole day. He'd always counted down the hours, the minutes, until five. Not drinking "the good stuff" until then somehow made it okay in his head. Although now that she was grown, Poppy'd figured out he pounded down beers all day because they were affordable.

"Pour your old dad a glass?" he asked her.

Is this a trap? He'd never asked her to pour for him before—probably because she never filled the cup to the brim.

"No?" her father said. "Alright, then." He shot up from his chair like a lightning bolt and it took her aback. She didn't know he could still move like that.

The door was only a few feet away, but she was frozen in place. Her muscles tightened up, held her hostage, but also braced for the hit.

He moved straight toward her, a dare scrawled across his face. *Don't move. Don't move.* She didn't know why, but it was a mantra being drilled into her head.

He came close, uncomfortably close, but veered away at the last second toward the old buffet where he kept an assortment of glasses and Wild Turkey. It was a game of chicken, and she'd won. "You want one?" he asked her as he raised the glass that threatened to spill toward her.

She shook her head. He'd never asked her before, and she certainly wasn't going to drink with him now. Surely it would be some kind of macabre toast to her impending marriage.

"C'mon. Have a drink with your dad," he said.

"You just got here." He took a long swallow of the amber liquid. "Haven't even sat down yet."

"I know, but… I can't drink. If I got pulled over, even if I was under the limit, my medical license would be taken away."

"Fuckin' pigs," her father said. He shook his head sadly. "Get you any way they can. Won't even let a doctor enjoy a drink after a long day. Fuck 'em all."

"Yeah," she said.

"Well, I won't keep you then. Go'n home. Walk her out," he instructed her mom as he fell back into the chair.

"Mom," she whispered at the door. The bruises were easier to see in the natural light. "What—come with me."

Her words shocked them both.

"Poppy! What are you talking about?"

"Just come with me. Please." She begged her with her eyes.

Her mother glanced behind her into the darkness of the house. "Stop being silly," she whispered finally.

"Mom! Come on. I don't—"

"You need to go," her mom said. "You're busy. Drive safe." She shut the door in Poppy's face. She was stunned, and stared at the paint-chipped door for a full minute before she retreated to her car.

What do you think you're doing? You can't even save yourself.

The drive home was blurred with tears. She knew she'd do a better job behind the wheel if she had a bourbon in her. The thought made her laugh, even through the tears, and a stream of snot bubbled at her nose. It was all settled in her dad's mind. Marry Will, or he'd make her mom's life more of a living hell than he already did.

He might even kill her.

29

RYAN

She didn't look surprised when she saw him slouched on her staircase.

"You look exhausted," he said, and immediately regretted it. Poppy's makeup was smeared, with streaks of mascara on her face.

"Ryan, I'm not in the mood for whatever you're going to say," she said as she pushed past him. He moved behind her as she unlocked the front door.

"Hey, come on," he said. "Let's go for a ride. Okay? You look like you could use a distraction."

She paused, the key still in the deadbolt. "Ryan, seriously. No."

"Come on, Pops. Please. A drive, like we used to. Remember when I got my first car?"

A flicker of a smile played at her lips. "The beast," she said.

"Yeah." She'd been more excited than him when he'd hauled home that turquoise Trans Am. It had taken him some time before he'd made the connection it was because she saw it as a faster, easier escape from her father.

"Just a short drive," he promised.

"Okay." She sighed. "We have to talk anyway."

"Sure. We'll talk—once we get where we're going."

"Not very long?" she asked as she looked up at him.

"Promise."

She rolled down the window and closed her eyes against the wind. Both of them knew where they were going, and no words were exchanged in the car. He pulled into the parking lot and they got out in perfect sync.

"It's beautiful here," she said as they sat on their bench.

He looked at her, soaked up all her loveliness. "Yes. It really is." Poppy blushed and looked at her lap, but he knew it was now or never. "Poppy, I have to tell you how I really feel, even if you don't feel the same way. It's worth the risk to me, the risk to our friendship. Because I'm falling—"

Poppy just held up her left hand. The diamond glittered in the sun, seemingly innocuous. How could such a little thing hold so much power?

He was shocked. "I thought you told him you were going to think about it. When did you start wearing it?" His heart plunged into his stomach. Sure, when Will had made that announcement at the cabin, everyone had started to celebrate, but Poppy had been quick to point out it was more a gesture than anything else when she'd emerged. A promise ring at best.

"That doesn't look like a promise ring," Sarah had said. He'd thought Sarah would be the first to squeal and make a big deal out of it, but she'd seemed wary.

"Well, I guess it's not," Poppy had said. She'd flushed and put the ring in her pocket. "We just… we're taking it slow."

"That's unorthodox," Penny had said sharply. Ryan couldn't figure out why she'd been so angry.

"That's awesome!" Mason had said. He'd been clueless about all of it. "Congrats, you guys."

"It's nothing," Will had said, backtracking. "Poppy's right. It's just a little token, I guess you could say." Penny had glared at him. "Ryan? Got anything to add?" Will had put him on the spot. Cornered him. And it was clear he'd loved it.

"If Poppy's happy, I'm happy for her," he'd said. Sarah had squeezed his hand and he'd squeezed back, thankful to have some kind of support. Poppy wouldn't look at him.

"So, I don't know if we're toasting to an engagement? Or what?" Mason had asked.

"No," Poppy had blurted out suddenly. Will had given her a look. "I mean, not like this. I don't want to make the trip about this—"

"We'll have a proper engagement party soon," Will had told them. "Let's just relax this weekend."

Poppy hadn't put the ring on the rest of the trip. It hadn't escaped Ryan's mind, especially when he'd talked to Eli. But he hadn't taken it seriously. Maybe he should have.

"Poppy?" he said. "When did you start wearing it?" he asked again.

"Just recently," she said. "At the cabin, half of my mind was made up to return it, but…"

"And?" he prodded.

"Will got to my parents, apparently," she said, and rested her elbows on her thighs. Her head hung heavy in her hands.

"Will went to your parents' place?" Ryan couldn't believe it. That little weasel had some balls after all. "When?"

"I'm not sure, exactly. Recently."

"How do you know? Did your mom call?"

"I went to see them. Today." His mind began to whirl. Poppy never went to her parents' house. The last time, when she'd taken him along, it had been months if not years since she'd stepped foot in that house.

"Why didn't you ask me to go with you?"

"I needed to do this alone. Actually, it was supposed to just be my mom there." That made more sense. Her dad was always at the bar, but Poppy rarely had the nerve to risk the slim chance he might come home.

"I would have gone with you." It was the only thing he could offer her.

She shook her head. "I didn't expect what happened there. I thought it would be okay."

"So, what did happen there?"

"My dad, he ambushed me. He told me that Will buttered him up by offering him a job, suggested it would be for someone famous."

"He's not famous," Ryan glowered. How dare that little shit bribe her parents? *Because it's the only way he could manipulate her, that's why.*

"It doesn't matter." She could barely get the words out, the tears choked up her voice.

"Poppy—"

"He's basically holding my mother hostage, Ryan. If I don't marry Will—"

"You can't let your parents be the reason you marry that smug asshole."

She cringed at the word, but didn't say anything. "You weren't there. You didn't see the bruises on her, didn't see how she wouldn't even look at me…"

"And you think marrying Will means your father will stop? You think after almost sixty years of abusing her, you, that he's going to magically see the light? It doesn't work like that, Poppy."

"I don't know! I don't know, Ryan. Okay? But what else am I supposed to do? I even—I even asked her to go with me."

His eyes widened. For all the years Poppy had watched the fallout of her father's beatings on her mother, she'd never talked about taking her mom out of the situation. *Not that she could save her,* he thought to himself. Nobody could. But Poppy even trying meant she was desperate. "What did she say?" he asked gently.

"She said no." She couldn't hold on any longer. Tears burst out like a dam.

For the past week, unless it was sex, he hadn't been sure if he could touch her. Now, it was automatic. He wrapped an arm around her and pulled her close. Poppy cried into his chest and he rocked her gently. She seemed so small, so frail, so unlike the utter everything she became in the bedroom. It was like there were two of her, the one who needed protection and the one who could do it all. He was the only one who got to see both. He was sure of it.

"You can't let that man control you like that," he said. Ryan stroked her upper arm and felt the hot tears soak through his shirt. He needed to keep her safe, wanted to be her shield from the world. Even if he didn't get to be with her, if they didn't end up together, he couldn't bear to have her sign up for a life with that asshole. "Not your dad, and not Will."

Poppy pushed him away from her. The look in her eyes had shifted. "You don't even have a father," she sneered. "You grew up in half a family, so what the hell would you know about it?"

Ryan stiffened and leaned away from her like she was poison. She'd never attacked him like that, not even during the worst days when they'd been kids. "I'll take you home," he said coldly and stood up.

He turned away from her and started to walk quickly to the car, but not before he caught the flood of emotions across her face. It was a nasty combination of regret, guilt and shame all at once, but he couldn't stop walking away. He'd had enough.

You tried to talk some sense into her, he told himself. He could hear her as she padded behind him. *And what do you get? She went straight for your weakness.* Poppy knew about Ryan's family situation of course, but had never brought it up herself. His father, or lack thereof, was his Achilles' heel and she knew it.

He hadn't thought it would sting so badly. But coming from her lips, it was cruel. Simply cruel.

Ryan got into the car and slammed the door. Poppy wasn't far behind. They both stared straight ahead, and Ryan was thankful he'd left the radio on. The ten-minute drive felt like it took an hour.

He pulled up in front of her building and slammed on the brakes. Ryan refused to look at her, to acknowledge her.

Poppy got out, but turned and leaned into the open window. Peripherally, he saw her open her mouth to speak, but he couldn't bear it. He stepped on the gas and tore away, even as the tires caught on the pavement.

30

POPPY

She huddled on her couch, spooning the last of a nearly-expired yogurt into her mouth. Two weeks. It had been two weeks since she'd seen Ryan, and it seemed like neither of them would give in.

Will's name lit up her screen. Poppy looked at the short message without tapping it so he wouldn't know she'd read it. *Email me doc*, it said. She rolled her eyes and shoved the phone away. *I'm not your assistant.*

Ever since he'd been cooped up in downtown D.C. with his new business partner, he'd texted her short, snappy messages like she was his secretary or something.

Her phone stared at her from the next cushion, taunted her. She picked it up again and scrolled to Ryan's name. But every time she thought about texting or calling him, she couldn't think of what to say.

I'm sorry? I wish things were different? Obviously, but what was the point in saying it? It wouldn't do anything, wouldn't fix anything. She sighed and tossed the empty yogurt cup onto the coffee table. The spoon slid out and banged against the glass, spraying little droplets across it.

"Stupid," she told herself.

She didn't even know what was true anymore. Will's ring hung heavy like the ball and chain it represented on her hand. She twisted it around, but it was no use. It seemed like she'd never get used to the strangeness of it.

Whatever. If she couldn't figure out a way out of this mess, she might as well check out for awhile. Poppy stood up and padded into the kitchen where she pulled a full bottle of white wine out of the fridge. She poured a glass and downed it in just a few swallows. Instantly, her head lightened. She poured another.

As she walked back to the couch, she pulled off the ring and let it rattle onto the table next to the dirty spoon. Curled back on the couch with her feet tucked under her, she sipped this glass a little more slowly. This was more like it.

Halfway through this glass, she heard the familiar engine of Will's Volkswagen outside. She glanced around her apartment and could instantly pick out everything he'd complain about. That her shoes were kicked off at the door instead of placed neatly in the closet. The pile of clean, unfolded laundry on the chair. *Who cares? It's not like it's his place.*

She counted each of his heavy steps outside. There would be thirty-four of them before he reached her door. Poppy had done this countdown so many times it was nearly meditative.

"Why didn't you answer my text?" he asked as he walked inside. He made a show when he pushed her shoes out of the way.

"Oh, I didn't get it," she said. He looked at the phone just an arm's reach away from her.

"You should keep your phone where you can hear it," he said. "It might be an emergency."

"You're absolutely right," she said, and took another sip.

"Poppy, you seriously need to start picking up after yourself," he said with a big sigh as he picked up the discarded yogurt container. "You can't live like a kid—what's this?" He picked up the ring, which had landed in one of the bigger splatters of yogurt.

"Ring," she said.

"I know that," he said slowly. "Why is it on the table covered in shit?"

She bristled at the word, but liquid courage flowed through her. "Because that's where it belongs." The words surprised even her, but they emboldened her. She felt invincible.

A darkness fell over his face. Without saying anything, he turned and slapped her. It was quick and sharp, the kind of surprise that took her breath away. Poppy jerked away from him and pulled her knees against her chest like a shield.

Will laughed, but it was unfamiliar. Mean and hard. "You know, when I found out what kind of family you were from, I admit, I was surprised. I thought I'd have to break you in... but it was clear from the second I stepped into your house that you know exactly what's expected of a wife."

She was confused. *What is he talking about?*

"And what happens when you step out of line. It was written all over your mother's face... and neck. And arms. Is she always so badly behaved, or did I just stop by at the wrong time?"

The shame that coursed through her was overpowered with sheer rage—and protectiveness of her mother. "How dare you," she said, and jumped onto the couch to leverage herself above him. She watched her hand toss what was left of the wine in his face. It wasn't much, barely a splash, and it didn't bring on the reaction she expected.

Will smiled.

The next hit was with his fist, far from a slap, and it knocked her off the couch. "You stupid bitch."

She felt her knee twist at an odd angle. From the floor, he looked ten feet tall. "Will—"

"Shut up. You want to know something? You want to know why I don't really care if you're a frigid prude or not? I've been fucking whoever I want, and you're too fucking stupid to even know."

She knew she should feel something. Jealousy, or anger, but she was numb. There was nothing. "Penny?" she asked bluntly. She didn't even care at this point.

"Among other people," he said with a laugh. "She's not really my type, but you know. Low-hanging fruit. Seems like you knew about her."

Poppy shrugged.

"And guess what else? She's not the only one, and that's exactly how it's going to be. Before we're married, after, all of it. And we will get married, Poppy, don't doubt that." He kicked her in the shin and she moaned as the sharp toe of his shoe shot pain through her entire body. Her pain lit up his face like Christmas.

"Will—"

"And you'll have my children, like a good wife. Just like your mom." The thought of having Will's children sickened her. For all these years, she'd thought she just didn't want to be a mom. Or wouldn't be a good mom. Maybe that wasn't it. Maybe she'd just been protecting innocent children from a nightmare like Will as a dad.

Maybe there's nothing wrong with you after all.

"And you'll learn to clean, and cook, and there won't be any more of this doctoring bullshit." Images of her mom flashed in her mind. She saw her on her hands and knees as she cleaned the baseboards religiously. Tucked into the tiny laundry room as she folded her dad's dingy underwear. Hunched over as she scrubbed at a worn-out pot crusted with the morning's breakfast. *No.*

"As soon as my script is picked up—"

It was like someone else moved her body. When Will bent over her with his fists clenched, she kneed him between the legs and felt the softness give. Even while her knee screamed in agony, a savage force tore through her. "You fucking bitch," he whispered, doubled over in pain. He clutched at his crotch and dropped to his knees. "Fucking crazy, white trash whore."

She overrode her own aching leg and the bruises surely already formed on her cheek, and pushed herself up. Poppy surveyed the room while instinct took over. *You have a few seconds. Just a few seconds.* People always ask each other what they'd take if the house was on fire and they only had one chance. But that wasn't fair. Adrenaline decides what you take, not your mind or your heart.

Everybody always said either their most expensive possession or their most sentimental. But that wasn't true. She reached from behind the couch, used it as a barrier in case Will suddenly recovered, and grabbed her phone and purse from the chair. It was her only hope, her only connection to the world without a monster.

As she raced down the stairs, she didn't care about the nosy neighbor who leaped out of her way. Or that she only had on boxers, a T-shirt and no shoes. "You okay, baby?" the woman called, but she was already halfway to her car.

Poppy only made it a few blocks before she pulled over to calm down. Tears tore down her cheeks, but she was already almost cried out. She looked in the rearview mirror, but for a second all she could see was her mom.

Her phone was almost dead, but there was enough battery left for a phone call.

"Poppy?"

"Sarah," she said. It was all she could get out.

"What's wrong? What's going on?"

"I… Will… he—"

"Did he hit you?" *How did she know?*

"Um. Yeah." She felt a release, just telling Sarah.

"Where are you?"

"In my car."

"Fucking prick," Sarah said under her breath. "I knew—come here. Right now."

"Sarah, I don't want to bother—"

"I said come here."

She hung up, pulled a makeup wipe out of the glove box, and wiped her face. Suddenly, she realized why this all felt so familiar, and she was five years old all over again.

When she was really little, her mom would grab her and take her out of the house at seemingly random times. Poppy was always terrified, with her mom's eyes nearly swollen shut and bruises already evident. "Come on, baby," her mom would say as she picked her up with superhuman strength.

They'd drive for what seemed like miles, but was probably only a couple of blocks. Her mom would clean up her face as best she could and turn up the oldies station on the radio. Poppy would sit in the back seat, scared until the soothing sounds of The Shirelles or Elvis lulled her into a dreamless sleep.

When she woke up, she'd always be back in her mother's arms, being carried into the house.

RYAN

The ringing phone bore through his sleep. Ryan pulled himself out of his hangover and reached for it. *Who's calling this late?* The last fingers of sleep and dreams let him go.

The time blinked at him right above Sarah's name. It was just past one. He considered not answering, but it was rare that she'd call this late instead of text—especially since he'd moved from breadcrumbing to ghosting her. He rubbed his head and glanced at the US Marshals application he'd completed earlier that night between sips of whiskey.

"Sarah, it's one in the morning," he groaned into the phone. "If this is a booty call, I'm not—"

"It's Poppy," Sarah said.

He bolted upright on the couch.

"Poppy? What's wrong? Is she—"

"She's okay," Sarah said cautiously. "But you need to come to my place."

"Sarah, tell me what happened."

"I can't… she's alright, but you just need to come. Now."

"I'm coming." He shoved his feet into some boots and grabbed his wallet. As he tore through the night, he ran across every possible scenario. *Please let her be okay. Please let her be okay.* He didn't know who he was asking, or if this was a prayer, but he willed her to be okay.

"Poppy?" he asked as he tore into Sarah's apartment. Poppy sat on the couch, her back to him. Sarah had her arms wrapped around her. When Poppy turned, she couldn't meet his eyes, but she didn't have to. Half her face was swollen and an angry violet hue.

"That fucking asshole," Ryan seethed through his teeth. "Your dad," he said. "It was your dad again—"

"Ryan—"

He gestured for Sarah to be quiet, and Poppy started to weep. "No," Poppy said through her tears, and she shook her head.

"No? If it wasn't your dad, then… Will?" He was incredulous. "Was it Will?"

Poppy didn't nod or say anything, but she looked up and managed to hold his gaze. Her eyes were bright with tears. Ryan sat on the couch behind her, sandwiched her between himself and Sarah, and hugged her close. "I'm sorry," he whispered into her neck. "I'm so sorry."

Even then, in that pained moment, she felt so good in his arms. So right. Like he could heal her and protect her from anything. Still, he kept up a barrier. *Don't take it beyond this, no matter how much you both want to.*

"It was my fault," Poppy said quietly.

"I, um, I'll let you two talk," Sarah said awkwardly. She slipped on a jacket and went outside.

"What do you mean it was your fault? Don't be ridiculous," he said when the door shut behind Sarah.

"No, it was," she said with a sniff. "Why did I let it go so far with Will? Why didn't I fight for what I really wanted? Why—"

Fight for what she really wanted? "Poppy, there's only one person responsible for this. And he's about to find out what it's like to be the one to take a beating."

"Ryan, stop." Poppy's eyes were huge as he stood up, and she shook her head vigorously. "Don't—"

Before she could stop him, he walked out the door and let it slam behind him. "Ryan?" Sarah asked as he walked past, a cigarette poised in her hand. "Where are you going?"

He ignored her and started up the engine. Sarah looked from him back to her apartment, confused.

Will answered the door casually, like somebody knocked on the door in the middle of the night all the time.

"The knight in shining armor. I've been expecting you," Will said with a smug grin. Ryan's fist pounded through Will's face smooth and fast. He could feel teeth give. "What the fuck?" Will sputtered through the blood that poured down his neck.

Wildly, Will tried to fight back, to land his own punch, but Ryan easily ducked out of the way. His military training took over.

Ryan hit him again squarely, in the neck. Will hit the floor where he gasped for breath on all fours. "Like the jackal you are," Ryan said. He kicked him in the stomach which dropped Will all the way down.

Will pushed himself onto his back, and Ryan was on top of him. He couldn't stop himself and hit him once, twice more. Will wiggled his arms free and held them in front of his face. "Okay, man," Will said through gasps. "You win. Okay?"

"It's not okay," Ryan said. Will looked up at him through busted glasses and what seemed like buckets of blood. He was broken, finished. Ryan could see that, and he stood up slowly. His hands ached and were covered in the warm slickness of Will's blood. *You've done what you need to. No more.*

"You have three minutes to get out. For good," Ryan said. "Get your shit, and get out."

Will scrambled like mad and gathered up his things. Ryan surveyed the room and breathed in. Poppy's scent filled his lungs. He noticed the ring on the table, but Will didn't even glance at it. Instead, he cradled his precious laptop bag in his arms like a child.

As Will moved toward the door, cowed down with his head heavy, Ryan blocked the doorway with his arm. Will stopped, dutiful, and braced himself for another hit. "The keys," Ryan said.

Will paused, and perhaps he even considered a lie. After a moment, he dug into his pocket and dropped Poppy's apartment keys in Ryan's hand.

Ryan followed him all the way to his car. On the landing below them, he saw the neighbor's curtains flutter. He supervised Will as the laptop bag was placed in the back seat. When Will got into the driver seat, the window was already down, and he somehow knew not to start the engine just yet.

Ryan leaned down and rested his forearms on the door. "I don't ever want to see you again," he said.

Will nodded, but didn't speak. "If I see your face again, or if Poppy sees or hears anything from you, you're finished."

Will nodded again and blinked hard.

"And I don't mean," Ryan said slowly, "that I'm just going to beat your pussy ass again. That would be too easy."

Will stopped breathing, but didn't dare look at Ryan.

"And don't think about doing something stupid. Like call the police and say you got slapped around a little. That's what you were thinking, right?"

Will didn't respond, but his thoughts were written across his face.

Ryan laughed. "You're unbelievable! You don't think all those bruises on Poppy's face have been documented? That there aren't already photos? Tell the police, and all it would take is them seeing one of those photos and you'd be done for."

Will's eyes grew big. *He hadn't even considered that. What a moron.* "But me?" Ryan said as he stretched his neck from side to side. "I'm not a big fan of the police. Not when things can be settled without their interference. You know? I said, did you know?"

"No," Will said quietly. His voice shook, like a little boy's.

"I figured as much. You're kind of stupid," Ryan said. "But just so you know, if Poppy or I do hear from you again? Or if you call the police? You know what will happen?"

Will was quiet.

"I said, do you know what will happen?"

Will shook his head.

"I'll find you. And I'll kill you."

Will sucked in his breath.

"Trust me, I have nothing better to live for than to make sure Poppy is free of you."

"I get it," Will said. "I get it."

"Good. Run along now," Ryan said.

He watched the car until the taillights disappeared down the street. Leaves crackled behind him, and he turned. The neighbor who'd caught him waiting for Poppy, the one whose curtains fluttered, was wrapped in a robe with her arms crossed over her ample chest. "You did good," she said.

"I don't know," Ryan said.

"I do," she said. Her hair was wrapped and she kicked at the concrete in pink fuzzy slippers. "Been watching that boy stalk that poor girl like she was some obstinate child for years. Couldn't do nothin' myself, of course. But it's good he's gone. You did her right."

"I hope so," Ryan said.

She put her hand on his arm. It was smaller and softer than he expected. "Don't doubt yourself," she said. "We all need some protecting sometimes. That poor girl… killing herself with her work. Lonely as hell, I could tell. I shoulda—I shoulda reached out to her."

Ryan looked at her sadly. "If anyone should have seen more, done more, it was me," he said. "I left her. After all those years we had, I just left her."

"Loneliness. Ain't it somethin'."

They walked back up the stairs together. The woman took his hand and squeezed it at her door.

Ryan continued up the stairs to clean up any traces of blood —and Will's presence. As he poured hydrogen peroxide on the splatters on the carpet, he drank in every piece of Poppy the room carried. Her favorite gray, wool jacket that hung on the hook. The aroma of sweet cream from her favorite lotion that lingered in the air. She'd used the same one since they were teenagers.

He rinsed the rag and dropped it in the washing machine. As he locked up with Will's old key, he couldn't help but think, *This might be the last time I'm here. Remember it all, every detail. This is Poppy's home.*

3 2

———————

POPPY

*V*oices in the living room stirred her awake. *Where am I?* It took her a minute to recognize Sarah's bedroom. Her face was swollen, puffy and painful. A headache started to throb at her temple as the painkillers from a few hours ago wore off.

Poppy groaned and rolled over. On the dresser was a display of framed photos. Prominently near the center was a snapshot of Sarah and her from years ago. They hugged each other tight and grinned into the camera.

"I don't know," she heard Sarah say in the living room. "I couldn't tell if she…"

Poppy couldn't make out what was being said as the voices rose and fell. She swung her legs off the mattress and flexed her knee. It was swollen and still painful, but it seemed like it was minor. *Thank God it's not a torn tendon or ligament.*

In the living room, Sarah and Ryan sat on opposite ends of the couch. "Hey, good morning," Sarah said with a smile.

"I've, uh, I've got some shopping to do. I'll bring back breakfast in a bit."

"You don't have to—"

"Really, I have some errands to run. I just wanted to make sure you were awake before I left. The spare key's here, okay?" she asked as she tossed a keyring into the bowl by the door.

Poppy walked up to her and embraced her. "Thank you," she said.

Sarah laughed. "It's no big thing," she said.

"It is." She glanced at Ryan. "Just a minute," she told him, and followed Sarah into the hallway.

"What is it?" Sarah asked as she hitched her purse up her arm. Poppy crossed her arms, barefoot in the vacant hallway and made sure nobody was around.

"I don't know why you're being so nice to me," Poppy said sheepishly.

"What in the world are you talking about?" Sarah looked at her quizzically.

"You know, you have to. About Ryan… and me…"

"Yeah, well, I'm not blind," Sarah said. "He told me last night. But, really P, it's okay. I wish *you* would have told me, of course. Before… all this—"

"I know," Poppy said. "I'm really sorry. I just… I didn't plan it. You know?"

"I know," Sarah said. "And Ryan and I, we had some fun. But that's all it was. I think we both knew that."

"So you're not mad?"

"Never," Sarah said. "But really, you two should go talk. I'll be back when the dust settles." She turned and loped down the hallway.

Poppy took a deep breath before opening the door. Ryan sat on the edge of the couch. He looked nervous. "Are you okay?" he asked.

She nodded and sat in the chair, suddenly shy. But he wasn't.

Ryan stood up and cupped her chin in his hand. His thumb brushed lightly over the bruise that flanked her eye. Even there, in Sarah's apartment and after everything, that little touch was enough to send sparks through her. "You look hot in that outfit," Ryan said with a smile.

She looked down and laughed. It was Sarah's old cheer-leading T-shirt from high school, and reached to just above her belly button. "There weren't many options," she said.

"I can think of a few options." He picked her up swiftly and swung her over his shoulder. Poppy squealed as he carried her to Sarah's bed and the shirt rode up to her collarbone.

"Ryan! Put me down," she laughed.

"As you wish." He tossed her on the bed and looked at her hungrily. Her bare breasts were exposed, and she moved to pull the shirt down. "Don't," he said. In one movement, he whipped the shorts off of her.

Ryan dropped to his knees beside the bed and placed her feet over his shoulders. Slowly, he worked his way from her calves to her thighs, one at a time, and kissed every bruise.

Poppy sighed and let her head drop back. When his mouth reached her mound, he kissed his way around up her hip bone and across her stomach. She moaned in frustration that he didn't even touch her where she wanted him most. As he worked his way up, he kissed the scattering of bruises on her chest she hadn't even noticed from the night before.

At her neck, his kisses became slower and longer. Finally, he reached her jawline and kissed along her cheek to the corner of her eye. "All better," he whispered. She pushed her pelvis against him, hard. "Did I forget something?" he asked her.

She wanted him, needed him, more than anything. He moved to roll off of her, to undress, but she couldn't wait that long. She unzipped his jeans and pulled out his heat, his hardness, and immediately slid it into her. "Poppy," he gasped, and she clenched him tight. Every thrust brought her close to orgasm. The roughness of the denim on her clit was a pleasurable contrast to her own slick softness. "Slower," he said. "Slower."

She obeyed, since she'd had a taste of what she craved so desperately. Ryan slid his hands under her and flipped them over. He didn't need to pull out of her, and suddenly she was on top of him. He reached down and unbuckled the remainder of his jeans and she rose up to help him slide them down. As he kicked them off, he pulled his shirt over his head. "It feels so good," she said as she bit her lip and let her head fall back. "You feel so good."

She looked down at him and memorized every part of him. She loved how he clenched his jaw when she took him all the way in, how he never quite closed his eyes all the way. Poppy reached behind and grazed his balls with her fingers, elicited a moan from him. "Come here," he said. "I want you to ride my face."

Poppy climbed off him, turned around and flanked his face with her thighs. He wrapped his arms around her legs and she lowered herself to his mouth. With her hands braced on his chest, she began to rock against his lips and tongue. His cock, wet with her juices, begged for her mouth—and she wanted nothing more than to feel his hardness against her tongue.

As she leaned forward to take him in her mouth, he slid a finger inside her and hit her G-spot. Poppy swirled her tongue around his tip and tasted his pre-cum mixed with her own sweetness. She could tell Ryan tried not to press into her mouth, tried to be gentle with her. But she wanted to take him all the way into her throat.

"God, Poppy," he whispered from between her legs. His finger still stroked her G-spot, but he whipped his head to the side and bit lightly into her thigh. Instantly, she missed his tongue on her clit and rubbed automatically against him, fucking his face, and he brought his mouth back to her.

Ryan knew her body like no other—even better than she did. When she got close to coming, he slowed down, removed his finger and outlined her rim instead. She never let go of him, couldn't get enough of tasting his cock. "Turn around," he said. When she stood on her knees, she almost fell, she was so weak from having him.

As she straddled him again, he guided himself into her. He filled her completely and she whimpered.

She'd never felt anything like it, not even in the prior times with Ryan. There was a freedom between them that made it even sweeter. They didn't have to hide anymore.

Ryan propped himself up and grabbed onto her thighs. When she rocked forward, took him in deeper, he licked and sucked at her nipples. "You're so wet," he told her. She held onto the bed frame and pushed him even deeper inside her.

She was on the brink, ready to come when he stopped her. Ryan held onto her waist tightly and commanded her movement. It was almost painfully slow, how he lifted and lowered her onto him—sucking and kissing her nipples, moving back and forth between each breast.

Poppy dug her nails into his shoulders. "I'm close," she whispered.

"I know." He released one of his arms and a wave of intense pleasure shot through her as he brushed a thumb across her clit. "Come with me, Poppy," he said, and moved his hands to her ass.

With his hands gripped on her ass, she rode him hard once more. Right as she was on the edge, he called out her name and spilled himself into her. The tremors brought her quickly to orgasm and she felt the now-familiar soaking between them. He pulled her head away from his neck and looked at her. "I love you," he said, his throbbing inside her bringing on another orgasm.

"I love you," she said. It was automatic, yet she knew that she meant it.

They lay sprawled across the bed, side by side. She curled into the crook of Ryan's arm and traced her fingers across his chest. "I meant it," he said, and looked at her. "I love you, Pops."

"You mean as more than friends?" she teased.

He laughed and slapped her ass lightly. "Yes."

"I love you, too," she said, and bit her lip. "But aren't you worried? About our friendship?"

"How could I be?" he asked.

"How could you not?" She brought herself onto an elbow and faced him. "I've been thinking about this fork in the road for weeks. Who knows? Maybe even months or years. It's not… you and I, it's not what I had planned. Or expected. I just… I didn't know what kind of future we'd have together."

"Didn't?" Ryan asked.

"Yes, and now? Now it's like there's a third option. It's not just 'the unknown' or Will anymore."

"Oh? You got another guy lined up in the wings?" he asked with a smile.

"Don't be stupid," she laughed. "I mean you. It's you."

"And do you think you could be happy with this path?"

Poppy grinned and kissed him. "I think so," she said. "I guess we'll just have to find out."

3 3

POPPY

*T*he next day, Poppy drove to the hospital, occasionally checking her makeup in her rearview mirror. Work normally put her in a good mood, or at least kept her distracted, but today she was dreading having to go in. She hadn't had time to get anyone to cover her rotation for her though. Between the fight with Will, her escape to Sarah's apartment and falling apart in Ryan's arms, and then what had happened after... Poppy felt her face flush at the memory.

Still, she thought she looked okay. Sarah had helped her conceal the bruising on her face with foundation and powder. The rest of the bruises would be covered up by her scrubs and the long shirt she'd put on underneath. That wouldn't attract any attention, no matter what the weather was like outside. Most of the hospital staff wore long shirts, even thermals, underneath their scrubs in response to the frigid temperatures set to keep germs at bay. *How convenient,* Poppy thought, rolling her eyes.

She pulled into her parking spot and turned off the ignition, pausing for a minute to take a few deep breaths. She checked the rearview mirror again. Sarah had skillfully applied makeup, but Poppy could still see the bruises underneath.

Oh well. Nothing to be done about it. She blinked back tears. *You cannot cry your makeup off right now,* she told herself sternly. A few more deep breaths, then she felt her pulse slow.

When she felt she'd regained some control of her emotions, Poppy got out of her car and walked into the hospital, distracting herself with the familiar ritual of attaching her I.D. badge and hanging her stethoscope around her neck. She caught a glimpse of the inscription of her initials on the bell of the instrument.

Ryan had given her the stethoscope years ago, when she had first started medical school. At the time, she'd rolled her eyes, thinking only of how many years it would be before she'd even need it. Still, Ryan had made her wear it, and had shown her the initials he'd paid to have engraved on the bell.

"If hospitals are anything like the military, people will steal your stuff in a second unless it's marked as yours," he'd commented, grinning at her.

She smiled at the memory as she walked into the hospital, then groaned inwardly as she spotted Penny in the hallway by the nurses' station. Poppy really didn't feel like getting into anything with Penny right now. She made a quick U-turn and took a back route to her first patient's room, scanning the patient's electronic chart as she walked.

Poppy recognized the patient, a diabetic teenager who'd come in a few times before, most recently with a concussion incurred during a blood sugar spike. As Poppy reviewed the chart, she felt her self-consciousness disappear, replaced by the authority of her medical training.

"How's the head, Cherise?" she asked.

The teenager grinned sheepishly.

"It's fine," the teenager replied with an embarrassed grin, "I didn't fall down this time, but - hey, doc, what happened to your face?"

Poppy sighed. Maybe her bruises were exactly as obvious as she feared. She decided to use sarcasm, that favorite weapon of all teenagers.

"I'm an MMA fighter on my off days," she replied, earning a grin from Cherise. "Are you still taking the meds I put you on last time? Tell me how they're working out."

A few minutes later, Poppy heard a knock at the door but, busy editing Cherise's chart, didn't look up. She only became aware of Penny's presence when she heard a small gasp.

Penny was standing by Cherise's bed, holding a cup of water and another, smaller cup with medications. She hastily averted her eyes when Poppy looked up, but not quickly enough to hide the shock on her face.

Poppy gritted her teeth. This wasn't the first time she'd had to hide bruises, but she hadn't done it since she was a teenager, and she had forgotten how embarrassing it was to be visibly damaged. If she ever saw Will again, she'd kick him in the balls for making her remember.

The thought made her feel slightly better. Holding onto it, she finished editing Cherise's chart, dispensed orders to Penny for bloodwork and medications, and moved on to her next patient.

The next few hours passed in the reassuringly comforting blur of hospital routine. Poppy hadn't run into Penny since, and nobody else had made any comments about her face. She checked her watch and decided she had time to eat lunch.

On her way to the doctors' lounge, Poppy saw Penny coming out of another patient's room. Before she could make her escape, Penny had zoomed up to her and grabbing Poppy firmly by the arm, maneuvered her into an empty room.

"What happened to your face, Poppy?" she asked without preamble.

"What does it look like?" Poppy fired back angrily.

Penny's expression softened.

"It looks like someone beat the living hell out of you," she said, gently touching Poppy's eye socket.

Poppy winced at the touch, light as it was.

"It was Will," she said.

"Will?" Penny's brow furrowed in confusion. "I thought maybe Ryan, or your dad. I mean, I can't believe Will would…"

"Really? You can't believe Will would punch me? Did he seem like such an upright guy when he was fucking you behind my back?"

Penny's mouth gaped open.

"Poppy, I'm so-"

"Shut up," Poppy interrupted her. "Will told me all about how he cheated on me with you, right after he gave me a black eye, and you know what, Penny? If you want that asshole, you are welcome to him, but just know that this- " she gestured to her face, "is what you might get."

Poppy stood there, breathing angrily through her nose in short bursts, waiting for Penny to deny sleeping with Will. To her surprise, Penny's face crumpled, and she launched herself into Poppy's arms.

"I'm so sorry, P," Penny sobbed, "I'm the worst fucking friend! I didn't know Will was like that! I just saw you and Ryan together, and it seemed so obvious you two were in love, and then Will... I mean, he made me feel sorry for him. I only slept with him once, and I felt so bad about it after, but I never, I mean, I had no idea he was like that. And your poor face!" she wailed.

Poppy tried to escape the hug, but Penny had some sort of guilt-induced death grip on her.

Despite her anger, she thought Penny was spot-on about one thing: she and Ryan had been in love. And she knew from experience exactly how manipulative Will could be when he put his mind to it.

"Can you forgive me, please?" Penny was asking. "I don't deserve it, but can you? And then we can go and find Will, and beat the shit out of him!"

Penny fumbled in her scrubs pocket, and pulled out a Taser, which she held up to Poppy's face.

"I can use this on him!"

"Shit! Penny, why do you have that here?" Poppy exclaimed.

"Because some of the people we get in here are so crazy!" Penny said, giggling.

"Uh, okay, I'm starting to think you're a little crazy, too," Poppy said, but she smiled at Penny.

"Maybe, but I'm still your friend, right?" Penny asked.

Poppy considered it. Penny had betrayed her, but she obviously felt terrible about it, and Will was, after all, a slimy, manipulative sleazebag. She couldn't really blame Penny for being fooled by him, not after he'd fooled Poppy for so long. She'd found Penny's offer to use her Taser on Will to be oddly touching, too.

"You're still my friend," Poppy replied.

Penny hugged her again, gently this time. Poppy's stomach growled loudly, making both women laugh.

"Let's go get some lunch before somebody comes looking for us," Penny said, tucking her Taser safely into the folds of her scrubs.

They were headed to the break room together when a scribe came up to Penny.

"Um, someone's looking for you," the scribe said.

"Who? No, never mind, don't tell me. The doctors will just have to wait until after I get lunch," Penny said, brushing the scribe aside.

"No, not a doctor. It was a guy. Not a patient, either," the scribe added unhelpfully.

Penny looked around and spotted Will standing outside of the staff lounge. She nudged Poppy, who spotted Will and darted behind a supply cart full of IV bags.

Penny walked up to Will.

"What are you doing here?" she asked him.

Will smiled at her. He'd taken care in dressing, had shaved and splashed on a costly cologne. More than a few female staffers eyed him as they walked by, but their glances didn't linger once they spotted the bruises mottling his face.

"I thought you might like to go out and get lunch with me, Pen," he said, reaching for her hand.

"I brought mine today," Penny replied rudely.

Will's eyes narrowed.

"Hey, I don't know what crap Poppy's been feeding you, but I broke up with her. The engagement was a mistake." His voice softened, and he added, "I knew she wouldn't be a good wife to me, and I kept thinking about you... we have so much in common, you know?"

"You and I have jack shit in common," Penny said loudly, causing people around them to stare.

Will tensed. Penny could see him struggling to contain his temper. More people were staring now.

"That white trash bitch got to you, huh? Well, fine. Whatever. I don't care about her, or you either. I'm having a script optioned by Netflix, for Christ's sake - I'll have more women than I'll know what to do with! I gave Poppy a huge ring, too, but it wasn't enough for her. It was enough for her dad, though. You should've seen his eyes bug out when I told him I wanted to marry his daughter. He had dollar signs in his eyes!"

Will laughed meanly and took a step toward Penny. By this point, everyone on the hospital floor was watching Will rant.

"I figured since she grew up watching her dad beat her mom up, Poppy would understand how to act right. But she never appreciated all I was offering her. My ring was in a puddle of yogurt, like trash! Then I thought, maybe she just needs to be slapped around a little bit to get it, ya know? So I gave her a black eye to match her mom's."

"Yeah? Looks like she gave it right back to you," Penny sneered as she gestured at Will's bruised face.

Will's face reddened.

"Call the police, Rob," Penny said to an orderly, not taking her eyes off Will, "and stay there, Poppy," she added, seeing her friend come out of hiding from behind the cart. A group of doctors came forward, grabbed Poppy, and pushed her behind them.

"You can call the police, but it doesn't matter. I'm never going to let that bitch go. If they arrest me, I'll make bail and find her. And if you try to get in my way, I'll beat your ass too, just for fun," Will sneered.

"Rob, please tell me you got that footage," Penny said.

Will's head whipped around in confusion. Rob waved his cellphone mockingly.

"Yeah, asshole, I got you streaming live right now. I bet that'll make your bail go up!"

"Not to mention the effect on his Netflix contract when they see this footage," Poppy called out from behind her human shield of doctors.

Will roared angrily and charged at Penny. Then he stopped mid-step and fell, convulsing, to the ground.

"Nobody touch him," Penny ordered, unnecessarily.

When Will finally stopped writhing, two police officers rushed up and cuffed his hands behind his back. Then they led him, cursing, into an elevator, while the entire floor cheered and hooted.

One of the cops, a tall muscular redhead, paused by Penny, who was hugging Poppy tightly to her before he boarded the elevator.

"Nice work, ma'am. If you get tired of nursing, you should think about becoming a police officer."

He winked at her as the doors closed, and the staff hooted some more.

"And you said I was crazy for bringing my Taser," Penny said, smiling at her friend.

"I was wrong," Poppy laughed.

"So, we're square now, right?" Penny asked.

"Almost," Poppy replied, "but you have to do just one more thing for me."

"What's that?"

"Help me pack? Ryan and I are moving to Newark."

Penny grimaced, "I hate helping people pack."

"Yeah, but you have to help. You're my friend," Poppy said.

"Damn straight."

34

RYAN

THREE MONTHS LATER

He picked up the last box and started downstairs. Poppy's neighbor leaned against the doorframe at the second landing. "She's lucky to have a strong man like you," she said as she held a wriggling little dog in her arms. "Moving with all these stairs, hell, I'd rather just stay."

Ryan smiled at her. "I'm the lucky one."

"Oh, Lord. Here we go," she said with an eye roll. "Nah, I'm just playing. Young love is a sweet thing."

He wedged the last box into the van, nestled between Poppy's other boxes and his own that carried what meager possessions he'd picked up since re-entering civilian life.

The neighbor had followed him to the van. "What you kids gon' do in Newark?" she asked.

Ryan looked at Poppy, plonked down in the passenger seat with the door open as her long legs dangled. He couldn't help but smile. *How did I get so lucky?*

"Ryan got a job with WitSec, and I got a new internship lined up. Miraculously," she said with a sigh. He smiled at her. She'd worried endlessly over whether or not she'd get that unexpected opening at the Newark hospital, but he'd known she'd nail it. She never gave herself enough credit.

"WitSec?" the woman asked.

"Witness Protection," Ryan said.

"Oh! Are you… you're the feds?" she asked.

"I wouldn't say that," he said with a laugh. "US Marshals. Not the CIA or anything."

"What about you, baby?" the woman asked Poppy. "What you gon' be doin'?"

"Working with kids with metabolic disorders," she said. "I never could decide all through med school between my two favorite specialties. It's nearly impossible to find an internship that covers both, and yet… here it is." Poppy held out her hands like she couldn't believe it herself.

He couldn't ever remember seeing her this happy before.

"Well, you kids be safe. God bless you both," the woman said.

As they went into her apartment for one last check, Poppy ran her fingers across the windowsill. "I can't believe this is it," she said. "It's crazy, but part of me is going to miss this old place."

"There's something to be said for the familiar," he said as he came up behind her and hugged her.

"What time's your mom arriving again?" he asked her.

Poppy checked her phone. "Her flight's supposed to arrive at eight," she said. "We should have plenty of time to get there before her."

"Enough time to stop in Wilmington for that deep dish place?" he asked.

"You're insatiable," she said.

"Only for you." He could feel her eye roll without having to look. "Honestly though, are you okay with this? Your mom staying with us?"

"I think so," she said. "Are you? I mean, I know it's awkward. We're just now moving in together, and she—"

He shook his head. "It's perfectly fine with me."

"I just, ugh, I don't know. Even with the restraining order against my dad, what if he… I don't know. And only eighteen months in jail, I still can't believe that. After all the years of hell he put her through—"

"It would have been a lot less without your testimony, Pops. That's just how the system works."

"I know," she said, as she stared at her cupped hands. "It's still not fair. And it took her so long to get over being mad at me about ratting him out… I just hope it all works out okay."

"It will." He spun her around to face him.

"It's just—I mean, she came to us because she had nowhere else to turn," she said. "That can't be easy, asking your own kid for help."

"She came to you because she loves you," he said. "You know that."

"Yeah," she agreed. "Maybe. I still feel bad about the whole thing."

"Don't you ever feel badly about it," he said, and lifted her face to him. "You did the right thing, a brave thing, and even when your dad gets out there's no way in hell he'll find her. Or you."

"Promise?" she asked.

"Promise." She looked at him with total trust. It was a responsibility he was happy to burden.

3 5

RYAN

When Poppy had told him she wanted to report her dad for domestic abuse, he'd wanted to support her—but only if she was really ready for it.

"That's great, Pops," he'd said. "But why now?"

"Honestly?"

"Of course."

"Because of Will."

Ryan had bristled. "What do you mean?"

"Some of the stuff he said to me that last night... I don't know, it put what my mom goes through into a new perspective I guess. I mean, it's not like I think it's my job to protect her. Or wasn't, at least. I know I couldn't have done anything as a kid. But now…"

"Are you sure you're ready for this?" he'd asked her. "Have you talked to your mom about it?"

"No," she'd said sharply. "I know she'll just deny anything's wrong, make excuses for him."

"It's going to be a tough road if she's not on track for it."

"Even if she gets mad at me, even if I don't know, she never forgives me… I know it's the right thing to do."

He'd beamed at her, and had been right by her side when she'd gone to the station in her mom's county to file the report.

"You got evidence of the abuse?" the officer had asked.

"You'll know when you see her," Poppy had said quietly.

The officer had raised her brows. "You know, that's not always enough. Not if she's not going to admit it—or press charges herself if an officer approaches her."

"It's all I can do," Poppy had said.

"And what about you? He ever touch you? Statute of limitations is going to be long past for you to press charges against him yourself. But if it goes before a judge, your testimony might be a big help… "

The officer had trailed off and looked at Poppy curiously. "Pops?" Ryan had prodded.

"Yeah. He used to hit me, too," she'd said quietly.

"You willing to go on record with that?"

Poppy had looked at the officer, then to Ryan. He'd nodded at her, told her it was okay with his eyes.

"I can do that," she had said.

"Alright then. Sign here. And here. We'll dispatch a car later today. This the best number for you? I'll give you a call when it's done."

Ryan had been impressed by how quickly the police had moved, but maybe that was how things happened in a small town. They never got the details of exactly what happened at the house, and Poppy never questioned her mother about it. All they knew is that the same day the police were dispatched to the house, her father was arrested.

Even though her mom had pressed charges, she'd still been at the police station and bawled as her dad was processed in the system.

Ryan was elated for Poppy, but it wasn't all smooth sailing. He'd been at Poppy's side when her mom had called the day after the arrest. "How could you?" her mom had screamed so loudly into the phone even he could hear her.

"Mom, I'm sorry! I did it for you! I didn't want to see you—"

"Why couldn't you mind your own business? What am I supposed to do now?"

Poppy had started crying into the phone, and Ryan had put a protective arm around her. "You want me to talk to her?" he had mouthed. He couldn't tell if she'd nodded or not, but she'd handed the phone to him.

"Mrs. Baker?"

"Ryan? What on earth… what are you…"

He could hear her mom try to pull it together on the other end of the line. Even then, with her husband in jail and as her daughter fell apart, she wanted to put on the show of the perfect housewife. "Poppy did it to help you. I know just how hard it was for her to make that decision. I hope you won't be mad at her for it."

"Ryan, thank you for trying to help, but this really isn't any of your concern—"

"Actually, it is," he'd said. "Now that Poppy and I are moving to Newark together, we—well, we wanted to invite you to come live with us. For as long as you like." Poppy had picked her head up off his shoulder and looked at him in wonder.

"What? Poppy didn't say anything about—"

"I know, I'm sorry. I ruined the surprise. She was going to tell you soon, but then things got a little crazy…"

"I see. Put my daughter back on the phone, please."

He'd handed the phone to Poppy, who'd put it on speaker. "Mom?"

"Poppy, is this true? Did you want to ask me to come stay with you—even before all this?"

Poppy had looked at him, questions in her eyes, and he'd smiled. "Yes, Mom. Really. We'd both love for you to come with us."

The other end of the line was silent. Finally, her mom had said, "Well, I don't know. It would be a whole lot of packing…"

"I'll help you, Mom," Poppy had said.

"Don't be silly, you've got your own entire apartment to pack—"

"It's not that much."

"And, oh, from what I hear, it's not going to be a trial but we'll still be going before a judge. I just don't know—"

"We're not moving for a few more weeks," Poppy had said. "I'm sure it'll all be settled before then."

"Well. Okay then. But only if you're sure. I don't want to be a burden—"

"We want you there. Really."

When they'd hung up the phone, Poppy had grinned at him in relief. "Thank you," she'd said.

"What are you thanking me for?"

"Everything."

3 6

RYAN

That was two months ago, and there had been a few more bumps in the road. Poppy had spent a full week helping to pack up her mom's place. It had been sentimental at best. Her mom had wanted to fawn over every item pulled out of storage, but Poppy hadn't wanted to keep barely anything from her childhood.

As Ryan looked around her empty apartment, he was amazed at how far they'd come. "Hey," he said lowly. "Last chance. One more tryst in this place? For old times' sake?"

She giggled and looked around. "There aren't even any curtains left!" she said. "What if someone sees?"

"What if they do? What are they going to do? Kick us out?" He pulled her closer and kissed her deep. "And besides, since when do you care if anyone sees? You've been an exhibitionist from the start." She blushed, but as always, she responded with her whole body.

Ryan unbuttoned her shirt and slipped it off her shoulders. "Naughty girl," he said as he looked down and saw she wasn't wearing a bra. Her nipples were already hard. As he unbuttoned her jeans and slid them off her hips, he hoisted her onto the kitchen counter. "Remember the first time we did this here?" he asked. He nibbled from her full lips down to her chin and across her throat.

"Mmm," she responded. Her shoes fell to the floor and he whipped the jeans off of her. "I want to watch you play with yourself," he told her suddenly.

"What?" she asked. Her eyes shot open. "Ryan! Come on, it's the middle of the day."

"You come on," he said. "Give me a show… show me how it's done." He stepped back until the fridge hit his back.

In nothing but knee-high socks, she pushed herself back onto the counter. Her legs were spread wide and feet perched on the edge. Poppy sucked briefly on two of her fingers and started to circle her clit. She never broke eye contact, even when her thighs began to quiver.

When she started to play and pull at her nipples with her other hand, he pulled his shirt off and unzipped his jeans. Ryan started to stroke himself as he took in her incredible beauty. She was completely shaved, her center bright pink and engorged. Even from steps away, he saw how wet she was. He'd give anything to lick her up and bury himself in her. *Not yet. Not yet,* he told himself.

Her eyes moved to his hand as he stroked himself a little faster. "I want to watch you come," he said.

"I want you…"

"Come first," he said. She dipped one of her fingers into herself. When she pulled it out, the stickiness left a string of wetness from her fingertip to her deepest crevice. She used it as lube and started to rub her clit even more furiously.

"Wait a minute," he said.

"Ryan, please—"

She stopped, but clearly wasn't happy about it. "Here," he said, and reached into the drawer to pull out a pink dildo she'd never seen before.

"You planned this!" she said with a laugh.

He shrugged. "So what if I did? Go on," he said. "I want to watch you use it."

She chewed on her lip and started to rub herself again. Poppy sucked on the pink shaft first, and he imagined it was him she had her tongue curled around. She reached her hand under her thigh and held the toy at her opening. "Like this?" she asked him with a smile.

"Don't be a tease," he said. She laughed and slid it halfway into her. "Oh, God," she said as she closed her eyes and let her head fall back.

"Look at me," he said, and she locked eyes with him again. As he watched her fuck herself, his cock began to throb. She pushed her groin against his gift and circled her clit with fervor.

"You're so gorgeous," he said. He could tell she was getting close, and her knees began to come together. "Spread your legs," he told her, and she snapped them back open. "Let me help you with that," he moved toward her and took the toy from her hands. He moved it expertly, and her whole body started to shake.

"Ryan," she whispered, "I'm coming." He pulled the toy out of her and she cried out. She squirted her orgasm and called out his name. Droplets sprayed his chest lightly, though he was several inches away.

"You're incredible," he said. He released his shaft to spread her wetness across his chest. She was limp and weak, but he knew her body. It would only be a few minutes before she was ready to go again.

"You didn't come," she said.

"I only come in you," he replied, and lowered his face to lick the arousal from her thighs. Whenever he got close to her clit, she shivered and he backed off. He'd never get tired of seeing her come. Every time, it was like the first.

Ryan dipped his head even lower and brought his mouth to where her lips hung over the counter. Just a few flicks with his tongue, and he encouraged drops of her come to fall into his mouth.

He stood up and loosely draped her legs around his waist. As he kissed her deeply, she transitioned from sleepy kisses to ones steeped in passion. When the tip of his cock brushed against her folds, she responded and dug her heels into his backside to bring him closer. "That's my girl," he said.

They both looked down at the small distance between them, and he slid his tip across her clit. She groaned. "How badly do you want it?" he asked.

"More than anything." She smiled up at him.

When he slid into her, it felt like home.

RYAN

They sat on the floor afterward, naked, backs pressed into the cupboards. "Do you think it will always be like this?" she asked. She sucked on an ice pop, one of the few remnants in the freezer they hadn't already consumed in the past weeks or thrown away.

"I think so," he said. "But there's only one way to find out." He reached over and surprised her with a drip of his orange freezer pop across her nipple.

"Ow! That's cold," she said.

"Here, let me help you," he said, and leaned over to lick the sticky sweetness from her breast.

She laughed.

"Hey," he said. "What do you think about this?" he asked, as he held up the red stick. "For next time I mean."

Her eyes got wide. "You want to—"

"Fuck you with a Popsicle. Why not?" he asked.

A glint in her eye sparkled. "When do you have in mind?" she asked.

"I'm ready whenever you are."

She looked at him hungrily. "With or without the wrapper?" she asked.

"Good question. What do you think? I mean… it might stay harder longer with the wrapper. But without, it would melt inside you and I could lick it out."

"You're always thinking about food," she said, and tapped him on the head with her own orange freezer stick.

"So, what do you say?" he asked. "I'll even let you choose the color."

"How gentlemanly of you," she said.

Poppy checked her phone. "We seriously have, like, ten minutes," she said.

"I can do two minutes."

She smiled and glanced toward the freezer. "If you're sure…"

"I'm always sure." He jumped up and pulled a purple freezer pop out.

"Hey! You said I could choose the color," she said as he nestled between her legs.

"I know. But then I remembered I'm the one eating it." He pressed his lips between her thighs, and she blossomed instantly.

She jerked when he placed the ice at her entry. "It's cold," she said.

"Shh, you'll be hot soon." He lapped along her lips. Soon, she eased onto the ice and started to moan.

"Good, that's good," he said. For a second, he lifted his head to watch her take it in.

"Don't stop," she said, and he went back to sucking her. Before he knew it, the stick was gone and her center was flushed a deep violet. Ryan lifted her hips and began sucking the juices from her. It intoxicated him, the hints of cold fruity juice mixed with her own heat and sweetness.

"You're so fucking hot," he said. She groaned, limp in his arms.

This time, when she came, it was the most incredible cocktail of flavors. He could have drank of her for hours.

"Ryan," she said as she caught her breath. They were sprawled across the kitchen floor, a trail of purple juice spread beneath them. "Seriously, we'd better get going, especially if you want to stop in Wilmington."

"It's not Wilmington I'm worried about so much," he said.

"Then?"

"I just want to make sure we get to the apartment in Newark with enough time to christen every room before your mom gets there."

"Ryan! You're crazy," she said as she reached for her discarded shirt. "Don't you ever get enough?"

"Of you? Never."

She rolled her eyes. "You seriously want to get it on in every room in the new place today?"

"Why? You think we need to christen the rental van, too?"

She slapped his chest. "I wouldn't put it past you."

"I'm just saying. I'm going to need to work off that pizza in Wilmington, and there's a pretty generous back seat."

"Come on," she said as she pulled on her shirt. "Let's get to the van before you have another crazy idea."

"You love my crazy ideas," he said.

"Well," she said as she bit her lip and looked down at the mess of purple on the floor. "Maybe that one," she said. The pink toy caught her eye, and she blushed. "And that one," she added.

"That's all?" he asked as he reached for his jeans.

"This is my favorite toy of all," she said and traced her fingers across his cock. He responded to her touch and started to get hard. "But let's go. The next adventure awaits."

She stood up and wriggled into her jeans. "I'm going to be leaking purple fruit juice for who knows how long," she said, and shook her head.

"Now how many people can say that?"

She laughed and grabbed his hand. Ryan turned around one last time to take in the apartment. It didn't look like hers anymore. Except for the stain on the kitchen floor, they'd erased all traces.

"What's wrong?" she asked as she locked the door and dropped the key in the landlord's box.

"Nothing," he said. "It's just kind of sad. You know? Besides the cabin, this is the first place we…"

"You're so sentimental!" she said. "It won't be the last. Plus, now we're starting a brand new adventure together."

He smiled down at her. She was right.

"Don't be sad," she said. "Remember that Robert Frost poem? The one about the roads?"

"Vaguely," he said. He'd never paid much attention in English class.

"The path you choose… it's what can make all the difference," she said.

She bounded down the steps ahead of him, and he watched her blonde hair bounce, and the curve of her hips with every step. Happily, he followed—to what, he wasn't sure. But he knew, with her, it was going to be amazing.

38

There's a little bit more of Connor and Sam, just waiting for you! Get this bonus story FREE — right now — when you sign up for Vivian's mailing list! Head to BookHip.com/QZXKAL for more info.

I know if you liked this book, you will LOVE the next story, HIS VIRGIN!

I'm rich, ripped, and hot on the campaign trail, vying for the highest office in the land.

She's a sweet little blonde reporter who is much too young for me.

I'll never forget the secret she whispers in my ear: she's never been with anyone before. That news almost derails me from my sole purpose in life, which is to smash every hurdle placed in front of me and win this campaign.

But I have to be good. No matter how long I stare at her or how much I fantasize about her, I can't even touch pretty little Meredith.

Except she defies me at every turn. She's a temptation I can't resist.

She's dangerous, a risk I can't afford… but her taste, her voice moaning my name over and over… I can't stop. Worse, I won't watch her walk away…

One-click His Virgin **now!**

CONNOR

Connor's mother hugged him tight. She smelled of that familiar blend of vanilla extract and fabric softener. "Bye, baby," she said. She held him out at arm's length as tears threatened to spill from her eyes.

"Mom, don't be sentimental," he said. "You act like I'm leaving forever. I'm thirty years old and have been on five deployments, and you're sad that I'm going to my fiancée's place?"

"You'll always be my baby boy, no matter what. And I'm sure your dad and Sean will be upset that you're moving out, too."

"Right, heartbroken," he said.

In his Mercedes-Benz, he revved up the engine and waved to his mom. She looked more like their housekeeper standing out front of the Georgian mansion, dwarfed by the soaring pillars. He angled the car out of the curving McLean neighborhood, and tried to shake off the dread that came from living with his parents and Sean again. *All three are miserable in their own ways,* he thought. *Thank God I'm out of there.*

Connor couldn't forget how many glasses of whiskey Sean had knocked back during his homecoming dinner out. "Think you ought to slow down, bud?" he'd asked him. Sean had given him a hateful look he'd never seen before.

"What, you're a SEAL for eight years, and suddenly you think you're in charge of everyone?" Sean had asked.

"Connor, don't be a prick to your brother," his father had said without even lowering the menu. "Some of us are trying to enjoy a nice meal out. Oh, can you tell me where your halibut is sourced? It's not frozen, is it?" his father had asked the waiter, who'd scrambled to satiate him.

His mom had done nothing but stare at her lap. *When did she get so depressed?* She'd always been emotional, but he thought returning from deployment would give her some sense of happiness.

He sighed as he turned a corner. A cyclist suddenly appeared, nowhere near the bike lane. "Jesus!" he yelled, and swerved into the suicide lane.

"Watch it, dick!" the cyclist shouted over his shoulder, speeding off down the hill in his padded red spandex.

Connor gripped the wheel, closed his eyes and counted backward from ten. *That's not an insurgent. That's not an insurgent. That's just an asshole,* he repeated to himself. He maneuvered the car back into the lane, and his heart pounded. For just a moment, as that flash of red had shot out in front of him, he'd reached for the gun in his ankle holster. *Maybe the therapist was right. Maybe you do need to stop being armed.*

But he couldn't help but see flashes of the war all around him. Last week he'd passed by a group of kids as they waited for their bus, and suddenly thought they were beggar children clawing at his coat. Just yesterday, the cashier at Capitol Supermarket looked exactly like the civilian in Kunduz who'd screwed him over for less than a dollar.

They were still everywhere.

Connor's phone rang, his father's name lighting up on the control panel. He pushed the talk button and the domineering voice filled the car. "Connor? Are you planning on coming into the office to finish up the paperwork today?" It was his annoyed tone, which came right before his raging lunatic tone.

Fuck. The papers. "Yeah, I'll be there this afternoon," he said. "I just need to stop by Sandra's for a minute."

His father sighed heavily into the phone. "I don't understand what you see in that girl. She's not quite up to par with what we expect of you."

"You haven't even met her," Connor countered, though he knew he was opening a can of worms.

"Met her? I don't need to *meet* her. Is she a member at Rolling Meadows? What does her father do—assuming she knows who he is? Where was her debutante gala held? You can't answer a damn one of those questions because she's nothing."

Connor sucked in his breath and gritted his teeth. His dad wouldn't get the best of him, not this time. "I'll be there before five," he said.

"You bet your ass you will. Connor, I don't understand," his father said. "I did all the work for you. All of it. Do you think becoming CEO of the country's biggest security firm was easy? And all you have to do is waltz in here, sign your name, and you're the COO of the company. You're basically heir to the throne, and you're pissing it all away on some piece of tail that doesn't mean shit."

"I said I'll be there before five," he said.

"Oh, I know you will. Because I'm sure Sharon is just bursting at the seams to tie the knot with her meal ticket."

"It's Sandra," he said, curtly.

"You just make one bang-up mistake after another, don't you? First the SEALs, now her," his father said with a deep sigh. "Although, you can't really compare the two. The SEALs worked out for you, but that was sheer luck. You won't be so fortunate this time around."

"Thanks for the vote of confidence," Connor said. He looked at the black screen of his phone. "I'm getting a call, I need to take this."

"Yeah, I'm sure it's wildly important. Don't be late," his father warned.

Connor's knuckles didn't return to normal from their blazing white color until he was safely parked at Sandra's condo. He jogged up the stairs, foregoing the elevator. *At least someone will be truly happy to see me,* he thought.

As he walked down the familiar hall, he pulled out the spare key Sandra had given him when he'd returned. "My place is yours," she'd told him with a smile. He debated where to take her for a surprise lunch. Luke's Lobster Penn Quarter, or maybe Bub and Pop's? He loved that she didn't need to be constantly wined and dined, unimpressed by his family's money.

When Connor walked into her condo, he froze at the door. A large man with skin the color of obsidian stood in the living room holding his shirt up to display perfectly carved abs. The man's trousers were at his ankles. Sandra was on her knees, going to town on the man's cock. Her red nails dug into the man's thighs.

"What the fuck?" he said, involuntarily taking a couple of steps back.

"Jesus," Sandra said, wiping her mouth with the back of her hand. "What are you doing here—"

"Who the fuck is this?" the man asked, yanking up his pants.

"Who am I? I'm her fucking fiancé," Connor said.

The man's eyes grew wide. "I'm out of here," he told both of them. As he squeezed by Connor in the hallway, he got a whiff of sex and L'Homme Ultime. By the time he turned back to Sandra, she'd already turned on the waterworks.

"Oh no," he said. "Don't you go turning this around—"

"Turning this around?" she said, tears gushing down her cheeks. She choked, struggling to find her words. "How can you say that? You can't even give me a chance to… to…"

"To what?" he asked. "Finish him off? Swallow? What are you trying to say, Sandra?" He leaned against the console table and hung his head. But when he closed his eyes, all he saw was Sandra once again on her knees.

"You're such a jerk!" she shouted while snot bubbled at her nose. "You only like me for my looks, you're always getting inappropriate with me, and now you're trying to make it sound like—"

"What the hell are you talking about?" he asked as he looked at her pointedly. The anger bubbled inside him and threatened to spill out. *Calm. Stay calm.*

"You barely know anything about me!" she yelled. "It's not exactly cheating when you know the other person only wants you to be a nice little military wife."

"What the fuck is your problem?" Connor asked quietly. The rage burned deep inside. "I come here and find you blowing some guy, and suddenly it's my fault? You're a real piece of work, you know that? My father was right about you."

Connor couldn't stop the words from coming. He hated himself, hated his father, and hated Sandra for doing this.

"What did you just say?" she asked, grabbing onto his arm. He looked down at those blood red nails and saw them digging into the man's muscled thighs once more.

"Take your hands off me," he said as he turned to leave.

"Connor! What about us?"

He turned as a mean laugh tore out of him. "Us? That would imply there was something going on between you and me. Which there isn't, as of thirty seconds ago. We're done."

"Wait," Sandra said. She shifted her weight from side to side. "What about... what about the ring?"

He glanced down at her left hand and saw it was bare. *Of course.* "Keep it," he said. "I can buy all the rings Tiffany's can make, but I can't buy loyalty." He wasn't sure, but he thought he saw her smile.

Connor raced down to his car, slid into the driver's seat and let his forehead rest on the steering wheel. *What the hell am I supposed to do now?* He couldn't get the image of Sandra working that guy's cock out of his head. *Is it going to become part of the reel now? The nightmare movie that plays nonstop in my head?*

He couldn't believe his father had been right. And what was he going to tell them? Already, the wedding preparations were in full swing. They'd booked the venue, the catering, and ordered the cake and flowers. Suddenly, Connor realized that *he* was the one who had put down the deposits on everything. Sandra had been playing him all along.

You're a fool, he told himself as he started up the car. He didn't know where he was going, but when he found himself en route to his father's company, he wasn't surprised.

Just like a kid, he thought. *Running back to mommy and daddy the minute things get tough.* At least his father would be pleased that he got to the office early.

As Connor walked through security, the female employees overtly sized him up. "Hi, Connor," one of the front desk girls said shyly. She bit her lip and turned bright red when he returned the greeting.

"Connor!" his father's receptionist said. She was a whip-smart woman in her fifties. "I wasn't expecting you until later this afternoon."

"Is my father here?" he asked.

"Not at the moment, I'm afraid," she said. "He had a lunch appointment. Did you need to see him, or is there something I can help you with?"

Connor looked at his father's closed door and sighed. "No, it's fine," he said. "I'm just here for the paperwork."

"Excellent," she said. "You know, your father is so happy that you'll be joining the company. Likes to 'keep it in the family,' he says. And I'm sure all the young ladies around here are pleased with the decision, too," she said in a low voice, giving him a wink.

Yeah. That's exactly what I need, he thought as he scribbled his life away.

ABOUT VIVIAN WOOD

Vivian likes to write about troubled, deeply flawed alpha males and the fiery, kick-ass women who bring them to their knees.

Vivian's lasting motto in romance is a quote from a favorite song: "Soulmates never die."

Be sure to join her email list to keep up with all the awesome giveaways, author videos, ARC opportunities, and more!

Vivian's Works

Married At Midnight Series
Forbidden Billionaire Romance
Deal With The Devil
Wed to the Devil
Vow to the he Devil

Sinful Fling
Sinful Enemy
Sinful Boss
Sinful Chance
Sinfully Rich

His and Hers series
His Best Friend's Little Sister
Claiming Her Innocence
His To Keep
His Virgin

The addiction duet
Addiction
Obsession

Other books
Wild Hearts

For more information....
vivian-wood.com
info@vivian-wood.com